LIMITLESS

The Terran Sea Chronicles

Jenetta Penner & David R. Bernstein

Reckless: Book One in the Terran Sea Chronicles
Jenetta Penner & David R. Bernstein
www.tormentpublishing.com
www.jenettapenner.com
www.davidbernstein.com

Printed in the United States of America

CONTENTS

CHAPTER 1

Sela

LAND.

The cool grass prickles my fingers as I press my hands into the earth. I lean my head back and my loose, red hair falls across my shoulders while the sun kisses my cheeks.

I inhale a deep breath as a slow breeze filters through the surrounding trees, the sprawling branches creaking and swaying.

Of course, Avalon isn't real land but, if I squint and look up at just the right angle, I can imagine what the world might have been like before Earth was covered entirely by water. The vibrant green leaves, the brilliant red and purple flowers, the strange delicate creatures flitting between them, quick as minnows but with translucent wings. The beauty takes my breath away—or is it just my gills betraying me?

The memories all rush back. Everything. Nerissa escaping. Cook taking Marius away after Nerissa injected him with a horrible serum that transformed him into a monster. One that was angry. Brutal. And, finally, how Jack cut off Marius's hand. How could he do that?

Marius's words, begging me to talk to him on the comm when my voice was gone, are like ocean waves crashing on the wounded, jagged points of my mind. I wanted to tell him that I loved him. Instead, he thinks I abandoned him. And I have no idea if Cook will tell him anything different.

And then there's Derya. My Sister—my dead Sister. I never should have let her go out on the personal watercraft. I should have told her to stay with the *Scylla*.

My eyelids close and tears begin to gather. My chest constricts as the weight of everything that happened presses against me, choking me.

I shove my hair from my shoulders and pull the thick strands into a tight ponytail, using a band from my wrist. When I'm done, I swipe at the tears that managed to escape my attempt at self-control.

"Sela," Una's voice crackles nearby.

I glance at the device sitting a few feet from me. Electricity bursts in my chest. Marius. Maybe the *Scylla* found Marius.

I stretch to grab the radio and tap the comm button.

"Una," I say, ensuring my voice doesn't show any emotion. Studying my hand, there's a sliver of brown dirt under my fingernails. Before now, I've only seen dirt in jars for sale at Cook's trading post or stuck in the deep crevasses between the jagged rocks of the Forgotten Boys' former Sanctuary.

"The *Scylla* returned from our last patrol," Una's voice sounds through the comm.

"And?" I ask.

The comm goes dead for a beat. "No sign of Nerissa or the *Echelon*."

Any hope that I may have had a moment ago wisps away. "Prep the *Scylla* to set sail in the morning. We're all going out again."

"Sela, we need to stop the search," Una says.

"Um, what?" I ask, caught off guard.

"It's been a week. If we were going to find them, we would have already."

"Exactly . . . it's only been a week." Anger burns in my chest.

"Listen, Sela. I get it." Her voice crackles on the comm. "I want to take Nerissa down, too, and I know you care about Marius. But we should be focusing on the people of Avalon, instead of looking for people who don't want to be found. This strategy isn't working. We need some time to think of a better one."

I scoff and roll my eyes. Not going to happen. "Una— you're not the one in charge," I snap.

The comm goes dead again. She's gone.

Adrenaline shoots through my veins. I push off the ground and bolt out of the park. At the edge of the natural setting, my feet hit the hard surface of a walkway leading into Avalon's urban sprawl. The concrete and steel structures of the settlement come into view. The small cityscape, lined with low living quarters, a school, and shops, can be seen from every vantage point.

In the corner of my peripheral vision, something whizzes by. I don't miss a step as Jack glides down from the air. Once his feet touch the ground, he falls into step at my side.

"I've been looking for you for, like, thirty minutes." His lips form a boyish grin.

I hold up my device. "You could have just used the radio. We have comms for a reason."

"That's no fun." His grin twists into a full-blown smirk.

Jack never flies with his radio. Lucky him, not having someone in his ear all day.

"It isn't fun when I can't contact you either." I scowl.

Jack shrugs. "Sorry. Bad day?"

"Same old thing that's been going on for a week."

He nods but doesn't press further. We've already been through this at least twenty times.

We pass two residents of Avalon going about their daily lives. One woman smiles and nods at us before the couple heads into a nearby shop.

Overseeing the *Scylla* is one thing, but the people on the settlement have quickly taken to Jack and me governing all of Avalon. Even though we're young, I guess our abilities make the residents feel as if we can handle the responsibility. It's strange and humbling at the same time. Maybe Una has a point about taking care of them for now.

"Updated status on the repairs?" I ask Jack, looking for another distraction.

"You, you could take a break now and then," he mutters.

I bump him in the arm. "My breaks always turn into work."

He nods. "Elijah is getting on with the senior Avalon engineers. He's having a little too much fun if I do say so myself."

I am glad Elijah is fitting in, but it's not the information I want. "What else?"

"All docks are secured again, and the technicians are working on the power systems. Elijah said the docks are nearly fully functional."

"Good," I say.

"Since we're almost up and running, have you thought more about settling into your own quarters now? All the Sisters have."

This isn't the first time he's asked me. I want to roll my eyes at him, but I feel his genuine concern.

"No," I say. "Avalon isn't my home."

Jack sighs. "I want to find Pearl just as bad as you want to save Marius, but these people need us right now."

I grit my teeth. "You sound like Una."

"I know how you feel," he whispers.

I arch an eyebrow. "Do you?"

"It takes everything for me to not just fly off in the night to keep searching for Pearl."

Maybe he's already done that and isn't telling me. But I would do the same thing if I had his abilities.

Jack stops walking, and I pause. He crosses his arms and locks eyes with me. "I promise we'll jump on any intel that comes in. But I need your help to secure Avalon and get life back to normal here. These people have been through enough."

He's right. The people of Avalon were treated like servants more than citizens during Nerissa's reign. She knew they had nowhere else to go.

"You sure you haven't been talking with Una?" I ask, focusing on the way the sun glints off his white-blond hair. It's better than looking him in the eyes.

"Well, Una is right. But no."

"Fine," I huff.

"Good," he says and gestures me forward. "Let's head over to the command center and . . ." He waves his hand in the air. "Oh, I don't know—*lead* or something."

I scoff at his silliness. But I know he's just trying to make me feel better. And I do. At least a little.

The command center is in the middle of the settlement. The five-story-high metal structure towers over the other buildings. To those inside the command center, panoramic windows provide a bird's-eye view of the settlement. Several comm uplink towers reach toward the sky, slowly turning, granting an opportunity to communicate with each other at all hours.

Through the main entrance, a buzzing of activity surrounds me. Avalon crew members sit at several stations, all tapping away at consoles while maintaining this gigantic floating city. With the repairs underway, the citizens are all hands on deck.

Most of the people we encounter greet us. Being inside makes me want to run back out to the open air. Enclosed spaces now remind me of my childhood spent being a test subject in Nerissa's experiments.

She will pay, I remind myself.

At the core of the command center, the blinking lights and beeping sounds reorient me to focus on the task at hand. There's work to be done here, and according to Jack, I'm a part of that.

"Jack!" Tug calls, swiveling in his chair and displaying a wide smile reserved only for his fearless leader.

Next to him is Ethan, another of Flynn's loyal Forgotten Boys. Ethan towers over Tug. He nods at me. "We still haven't located the vessel that Mateo, Cyrus, and Riley stole." His lip curls as he speaks their former leader's name.

I glance at Jack. How is he going to react this time?

As expected, Jack's jaw clenches. "He had every chance to be my brother and help bring Avalon back to life. But I better not see that coward and his misplaced ego again. If I do, I will fly him out to sea and float him."

"What do you wanna do then?" Tug asks, bouncing on his heels. "Are we goin' after him? I'm ready."

Ethan drops a hand onto Tug's shoulder, settling him. Jack waves them closer. Ethan goes to his side, pulling Tug with him.

Ethan relays something to Jack, but the whole thing is just a bunch of mumbling to my ears. I try to listen, but my mind wanders back to Marius. He should be with us right now. With Marius by my side, maybe I would already be settled on Avalon. The thought makes the walls close in tighter. I need to get out of here.

"You have everything under control," I call out to Jack. Joining their little group of Mateo-haters isn't on my agenda.

Jack glances over his shoulder at me and his eyebrow arches in question.

I force a smile, attempting to reassure him. "I have some . . . things to do."

With that, I spin toward the exit and push down the urge to bolt from the command center, so Jack doesn't see and follow me. I place one foot in front of the other and draw in a slow breath, all the while counting my heartbeats and willing their pace to slow.

Each step I take pounds in my head like storm waves against the hull of a ship. I just need some time to think.

Out of sight of the command center and unable to hold back my urge to escape any longer, I break into a sprint, zigging between structures and zagging through countless alleys. A few people try to stop and talk to me, but I ignore them.

The ocean calls to me like a relentless siren. No one visits the outer rim of the settlement since the drop is at least ten stories high and most people want to get away from the water, not closer. Perfect.

Over the side, the waves crash against the settlement's metal walls, as if the Terran Sea wants to climb up and swallow us too, as it has every other surface of the world.

My breath hitches at the steep drop and I suck in a lungful of briny air. Water sprays over me as the wind rushes up from below. The need to make everything right again propels my legs forward. And I dive into the air, driving my body down toward the water that connects Marius to me.

CHAPTER 2

Jack

FLYING WILL BE faster, I said. More efficient, I said. No problem at all, I said. Now here I am, fifty feet above the docks and every trusting head, carrying a steel crate full of heavy parts that's slowly slipping out of my sweaty hands because, unlike me, the crate was never subjected to Nerissa's antigravity experiments. My muscles burn, but I tighten my grip. I'm not going down in history as the Avalon leader who dropped a generator on his citizens.

I grit my teeth. The dock isn't much farther, and I focus on landing as close as I can to the crates already stacked there.

A bead of sweat rolls down my forehead and into an eye. I grumble and blink my vision back into focus.

The second my feet touch the dock, I throw down the crate, and the parts rattle against each other. Hope nothing broke. I flex my numb fingers and blood rushes in, bringing some feeling back to each appendage.

Only two more crates. I start to lift off again, but instead drop onto a box and take in a deep breath. No need to be a martyr.

"Jack!" a female voice calls out.

I cringe. Can I hide? I pop up. No. She's already seen me. I suck in a breath and face the only female member of the Forgotten Boys.

"Hi, Coral."

Her long, dark brown hair is tied back and swishes behind her like a tail. The awkwardness between me and Coral has been my constant companion since the moment I fell for Pearl.

"Hey, Jack. What's going on? Haven't seen you in a few days."

"Oh, nothing," I say, wondering how I can get out of this conversation.

"Doubt that." She smiles. "You know you can talk to me."

"Yeah, sure." I gaze up at the sky. *Think she'd notice if I just took off?*

"So, heard anything about Pearl?" She chews her bottom lip.

I clear my throat. "No."

I really need to go before this gets weird.

Coral lays her hand on my shoulder and squeezes. "I'm here for you, Jack."

Too late.

I study her face. The familiar scowl isn't present, but I know her well enough. If Pearl had never come along, things might have ended up different for me and Coral. At least in Coral's eyes.

I pull away, not wanting to give her the wrong idea. Her lips tug downward, but within seconds, she flips the expression over into a grin.

I narrow my eyes. I'm used to her sarcasm, especially when it comes to Pearl. But something is up, and I'm not falling for the fake smile.

"Listen, Coral. Nothing has changed. I'm not giving up on Pearl. Ever."

She twists away from me with a huff.

I grind my teeth together. "I'm sorry—"

"It's fine," she snaps and then stomps away. The echo of her boots hitting the deck resonates in my ears.

It's nothing against you. I would bet my life that she would clock my jaw if I said that last thought out loud. Instead, I kick the corner of a crate and pain zings up my toe. A curse escapes my mouth.

The pain fades as something zips up to me from the side. Nyx!

"No way! Did Elijah fix you? I love that kid!"

The pain in my toe—and in my thoughts—dissipates at the sight of my favorite AI drone in the entire world. I reach out for her, but she flits around me, buzzing, her eyes shifting between a bright yellow and green glow.

I laugh. Nyx is just as excited as I am.

At least today isn't a total waste.

"Come here." I snag her, and she nuzzles into my shoulder, letting out little chirping sounds. "Good to see you too."

She continues to chirp, and her emotion colors aren't settling down.

I hold her at arm's length. "What's up, Nyx? You're not still malfunctioning, are you?"

She squirms away from me and then comes back, repeating the cycle two more times.

"I think I should take you back to Elijah—"

She groans and the sensors in her eyes turn to slits. Something about the expression reminds me of one Coral would throw in my direction.

She flies away again, farther this time.

Wait a second. She wants to show me something.

I lift off the ground and follow her. Nyx's small but strong white frame is far ahead of me, her thin metal wings flapping intensely. I push myself to keep up.

I grab a last look at the dock. Meh—the job can wait. Nyx wouldn't take me somewhere if it wasn't important.

She zips toward one of the taller residential buildings and hovers near the entrance.

I land on the ground next to her. "This is what you wanted to show me?"

Her lights flicker.

I shrug. "OK, better be good. Or else you're going back to Elijah."

Her eyes form slits again and she crosses her tiny arms over her chest. A little huff emits from her internal sensors.

"Fine, fine," I relent.

In an instant, she lets out a buzz and turns toward the door, activating it. She zooms into the building and takes off again.

I race after her and jog up the stairwell. We pass a couple coming down the stairs, and both duck as Nyx nearly clocks them in the head. The guy's eyes widen and his girlfriend or whatever squeaks in surprise.

"Sorry!" I say and push past.

I stifle a laugh into my hand. Their faces were priceless.

Nyx waits at a door to the second floor, tapping her foot on the air.

I open the door and, once again, she flies through, leaving me in her wake.

Within seconds, we arrive at our destination in front of one of the apartments. Number 10.

"Why did you take me here?"

Nyx's large, eager eyelike optics turn a soft teal.

"Am I supposed to know someone here?"

She flutters up and taps on the door with her little fist, gesturing for me to move closer with the other.

I fold my arms across my chest. "OK, fine. I'm curious now."

I knock on the door, hoping I'm not bothering some girl who's taking a shower . . . well, on the other hand . . . *Stop it, Jack*, I scold myself.

Nyx buzzes close to the doorknob.

"No way. I'm not opening someone's door without their permission. I'm trying to be a leader, not a burglar."

She nudges my hand forward.

I give in and turn the knob. Cautiously, I lean through the small opening. "Hello! Anyone there?" *My crazy AI wants me to break into your apartment.*

I wait a few seconds before I call out again. No one.

"You better not get me into trouble. People actually trust me now."

Her lights flicker and she waves me forward.

Smirking, I stroll inside.

It's a studio like my own, with a bed in one corner, a small kitchen close to the door, and a small divider near the bathroom.

Nyx zips across the room.

The hairs on the back of my neck stand up. It's ridiculous, but there's something about this unit. Everything is tidy and in place. The bed is perfectly made without any wrinkles in the blanket. Must be a temporary residence.

"You know who lives here?"

Nyx hovers over the small table next to the bed. But the glare of the sun through the single window blocks my view of what she's interested in.

On the table sits a white flower with a yellow center. I reach for it, my hand shaking, and lift the plastic hair clip from the table.

"Pearl lived here." My heart sinks into my chest, and I struggle for breath.

The back of the flower has a clasp. I flip it open, imagining Pearl doing the same and then running the barrette through her hair.

This is the room from the video Nerissa made me watch. I walk toward the kitchen, the clip firmly in my hand, and inspect every surface. Trailing my fingers over the length of the countertop, I almost feel Pearl's arms around me again.

Nyx zips around the room like she's found something else. This time, I don't doubt her. She was a former security drone and that programming must have led her to this place somehow.

"What is it?" I ask.

She hovers near a small display screen. It comes to life with Nyx's touch. The screen flickers for a moment and then settles in before several lines cascade across the panel.

I tap the screen and nothing changes. Damn it, if this is Pearl's, I *need* it to work.

Her face pops up on the screen, and I step back, my leg bashing against the oversized chair in the center of the room.

Bringing a shaky hand to my forehead, I stare at her. I never forgot what she looked like. But seeing her face so close to mine again takes my breath away, just as it had the last time I saw her.

I scramble toward the screen again and trace my finger across the glass, outlining her beautiful face.

Remembering Nyx, I glance around the room. She sits on a small shelf, her eyes glowing blue as if she's feeling the same emotions as me.

A link at the corner of the screen blinks green.

One message. I stare at the words, my finger hovering over the link. Pearl left a video message, but I can't bring myself to press play.

Instead, I sit there feeling the energy between the space of my finger and the glass. My eyes dart between the words and her face.

The need for information finally overpowers the ache in my heart, and I drive my finger toward the small triangle next to the words.

Pearl comes to life, sitting in the same chair then as I am now. She straightens her spine and takes a breath.

"Jack," she says, and my entire body freezes.

"I know you're coming back for me." She stares into the camera, but it feels like she's looking straight into my eyes. The rest of the world fades to black. Nothing else exists. Only her.

"I just have to hold on a little while longer. This is probably stupid." She laughs and the sound rips through my body. I gasp as if I'm plummeting from the sky toward the ground. "You're going to make fun of me for a video journal. Once you get back, I know I'm going to hear it." She pauses and glances at her hands. "This helps, though. Talking to you. I miss you so much."

She reaches forward, and the video pauses.

No, no, no. I leap from my seat and grab for her. "Don't go!" The words escape my mouth.

My chest clenches with embarrassment, and I fall back into the chair with a thump. I glance at Nyx, still on the shelf. Hearing Pearl speak about me in that way sends a shiver down my spine.

Glancing at the screen again, the title of the video appears at the bottom. I lean closer and flick my finger across the smooth surface. "Video journal number one. Maybe there's a second one?"

Even better than a second one, a list of video file names floods the screen. Excitement clouds my mind, and I want to watch the most recent one. No, better to go in order. Who knows what clues she could have left?

In the next video, Pearl wears my favorite sundress. The yellow floral patterns blend with white and soft pinks in the background of the fabric. No one would ever peg me as a guy who would notice that type of thing. But with Pearl, everything is different. My gaze falls to the flower clip in her hair, the same one still clutched in my hand. Why can't she be here for real?

The message of this video is pretty much the same: she misses me and wants me home.

No way would I ever make fun of her for recording these.

Part of me dreads watching the rest; seeing her pain only increases mine. But I do anyway. As they go along, the messages get shorter and shorter. A pit forms in my stomach as dark circles form around Pearl's eyes, and her face becomes scarily gaunt.

My chest aches in desperation. By the time I get to the last video, Pearl is only a shadow of the girl I love.

She's not even looking at the camera. Instead, she stares at something next to her. I glance in the direction of where she was looking, but there's nothing there other than the smooth floor.

"I was stupid to do this." Her breath hitches, as if she's holding back tears. "It's been too long. You should have come back by now. Having hope for your return was foolish. Who knows if you're even alive." She shakes her head and closes her eyes. Several of the tears she was holding back snake down her cheeks. I reach to her out of habit, needing to wipe her sadness away, and then pull back to wipe at my own eyes.

It's only then that she turns to the camera and looks at me through the lens. "I won't be making any more videos after today. It hurts too much to speak to you as if you're here. Jack, I hope you're free and living your life. Even without me."

The screen freezes on her blurry face.

Heat flushes through me and the muscles in my legs twitch, begging for me to escape to the sky. Pearl's voice rings in my head as I sprint out of the unit, down the stairs, and finally out of the building's door and into the wide-open air.

Leaning over, I press my hands into my thighs. I struggle for breath.

Nyx zips by me. "Leave me alone!" I shout and jet up into the sky. The sound of her buzzing fades as I climb higher and higher.

Even without me.

"All I want is to find you!" I shout. I don't blame her for giving up hope. But hearing the words from her lips adds an extra sting to my already battered heart.

I gasp as thin air hits my lungs and then slip as my connection to gravity weakens. Instead of fighting it, I drop and hover at a lower altitude, wallowing in the silence around me. The ghost of Pearl's voice echoes in my head.

The Avalon settlement is a blip on the vast Terran Sea. No wonder Pearl lost all hope.

Is looking for her a lost cause? Is *she* even alive? Part of me wants to plummet into the ocean with these thoughts.

Distant buzzing interrupts my thoughts. Far below, Nyx's flickering eyes turn every shade of color. She rises and falls quickly, trying to follow me.

"Go down!" I shout at her.

But she doesn't even waver—always loyal.

I draw in as much air as I can as my head lightens. Losing Pearl is enough, losing Nyx is another thing. I don't want her to get damaged again, this time because of me.

Dropping down, I grab her and pull her close. "You never give up, do you?"

Her eyes stop flickering and turn bright white.

I furrow my brow. "What are you doing?"

The altitude might be glitching her. We fall to a safer level where the pull of gravity is stronger. Her comm device clicks on, and a familiar voice filters out of her speakers. I choke on my next breath.

"Flynn," Marius says, causing my blood to run cold.

The last time I saw Marius, he was in a Nerissa-injection-induced rage and I had to go do something stupid like cut off his hand.

"I have your precious Pearl," he continues. "If you want to see her alive again, you will meet me. Alone." He rattles off a set of coordinates, and then the message starts over again.

My lip curls over my teeth. Our last encounter flashes to the forefront of my mind. Sela's boyfriend or not, he's going to regret threatening me and the girl I love.

CHAPTER 3

Sela

BEAMS OF SUNLIGHT cut through the water, casting wavy lines of light to filter down into the water. My hair swirls around me in the warm depths, and I push the strands away from my face, taking in the scene around me. The beautiful blue and teal of the ocean's surface above fades into darkness just below my feet.

I lean back, close my eyes, and let the sea flood me with memories of home.

"Sela?" my father's deep voice calls from a far back corner of my mind.

"Yes, Papa?" An eight-year-old version of myself emerges from under a cascade of vines growing in one of Atlantis's hydroponic garden wings.

My father crosses his arms over his wide chest. "We've been looking for you all afternoon. You didn't show up for your tutoring."

All the standard excuses whirl through my child mind but, in the end, the truth exits my mouth. "I miss Mama," I whisper.

Papa's stance softens as he sighs. Then he bends down and opens his arms to me. Without hesitation, I race down the aisle of plants and into his embrace. I press my cheek into the roughness of his thick graying beard. Not that I've ever liked it, but today the familiarity brings comfort into my lost child's soul.

"I miss her, too, little minnow," he says in a gravelly voice as if he's holding back tears.

I pull away and look him in the eyes. "Why did she have to die?"

Papa breaks my stare and shakes his head. "I can answer many questions, but that's not one." Sadness pools in his eyes. Gently, he touches my hair, the color I shared with Mama. "You are so much like her." With those words, he stands and pats me on the head. "I'll inform your tutor that there will be no school today."

I open my mouth to ask if he would spend the rest of the day with me since he's always working. But, before I get the chance, he cuts me off.

"Now I must get back to my duties. What if you invite Marin and Derya over for the afternoon? I'll make sure someone sends up a snack for you three."

I nod. I guess it's fine so long as I don't have to invite Una too. She's older and bossy. "Can I invite Talise?"

"Sure." He waves his hand in the air to motion me toward the exit. "But only if you go now."

I wrap my tiny arms around his waist and give him a quick squeeze. Then I race for the automatic doors, and a rush of warm wind hits my body as the door whooshes open.

The sensation jolts me into reality, and I inhale a gulp of water through my neck gills. My eyes fling open, and I shake my head. Bubbles form all around me as the memory stings in my mind and chest. I need to get back to work.

As I push to the surface, my insides warm to the change in temperature. Nothing in the water affects me anymore. Although I usually feel like what Nerissa did to me is a curse, Marius was right: it is often a gift. If only the abilities weren't forced on me. So many others had to die in her horrible experiments for mine and Jack's abilities to succeed.

Gritting my teeth, I kick my legs harder and burst out of the water. After my vision clears, I search for Avalon. But the settlement is only a hazy mass on the horizon. I need to pay better attention next time to the flow of the undercurrents, so I don't end up lost at sea.

After a few minutes, I reach the north side and grab onto one of the access hatches to pull myself up onto the landing. I jiggle the handle, but it doesn't budge. I make a mental note to memorize the access codes. I suppose jumping off the settlement for some alone time has consequences.

The rush from diving into the water is gone as I grip each metal handhold and climb. My hair is heavy, weighed down by water. Though, I'm not out of breath when I reach the top. Just annoyed at my lack of planning.

Wrapping my hand around my hair, I twist the long locks and squeeze out as much of the water as I can before heading off toward the comm tower.

If there is any information about Marius, I'll find it there.

When I arrive, there's already a group gathered around one of the radio stations. Una, Tug, Marin, and Ethan surround a guy I've never seen before. He seems to be one of the tech officers. My friends don't even notice as I walk through the door.

"What's going on?" I ask.

Una and Marin whip around to face me. They glance at each other, not saying a word.

"What?" I press.

Una lets out a long breath. "We intercepted a looping transmission sent to Jack's drone."

"What did it say?"

Una twirls her finger at the tech guy and moves out of the way. I push past her to listen. My chest clenches as Marius's voice filters out from the station.

Once the message ends, I ask the tech guy to repeat it. He moves his fingers over the station, starting the message again.

"Has Jack heard this?" I ask.

"Elijah fixed Nyx," Tug says, rocking in his swivel chair. "She would have found him already."

"No one has seen him?" I ask the group. "Or bothered to look?"

"Uhh . . ." Tug says.

Ethan shoots him a glare.

My stomach drops. "Have any docks been accessed?" I ask the tech guy. Jack can't fly to those coordinates. It's too far.

Una steps forward. "Sela—"

I put my hand in the air to stop her. I can't believe someone didn't find me after listening to this.

"The east dock. Someone accessed it almost twenty minutes ago," he says.

I whirl around on the others. "No one thought to check for Jack?"

They stare blankly at me.

"We just found out too," Marin says.

If it were anyone else, there would have been an alarm. But Jack and I have access to everything on Avalon. He knew that.

I bolt from the room, ignoring Una and Marin as they call after me. There's no time to talk this over.

Making my way through the busy shopping and commercial district, I weave through an area more congested with people.

"Sorry!" I shout several times over my shoulder.

Once the crowd thins, I pick up my pace again and dart through the service alleys, avoiding the heat that's radiating off the power conduits lining this part of Avalon. A minute later, I arrive at the elevator shafts and signal a cab to take me down to the open-air docks.

Descending, the doors open, and then I walk toward rows of boat ramps lining a long metal harbor that rest in a large alcove, one surrounded by Avalon's towering walls. I spot Jack across the way and let out a relieved breath. "Jack!"

His eyes meet mine as I run over to him, but his pinched expression is not conveying relief, more like annoyance.

Next to him, a small scout vehicle is already packed with supplies and several weapons. It's not much more than a glorified dinghy—big enough to hold one person and gear. Nyx buzzes around Jack's head in what looks like agitation and excitement.

Two little lines form between Jack's eyes. Without a word, he goes back to packing.

I scoff. "You were just going to leave, weren't you?"

"I don't have a choice."

"Of course, you have a choice." My lips thin into a straight line.

"Nope. Not if I want to see Pearl again."

I throw my hands in the air. "If the tables were turned, I wouldn't leave you to go off and rescue Marius. We would make a plan together."

Jack continues tossing in jugs of water and rations. "Sela, you're not coming."

"You don't get to make that decision for me, Jack." I grab one of the rifles from the dock and toss it into his ship. He's planning on a fight with all the firepower he's bringing.

"What are you doing?" he asks.

"What does it look like? I'm coming with you."

Jack rubs a hand over his face. "No, this isn't going to work. I'm going alone."

"You know as much as I do that this is a trap. You need me."

"Sela, *please*."

When I don't respond, he clenches his jaw and then jerks the water jugs out of my hands.

Several dock slips away, the *Scylla* floats, waiting for its captain. "Fine, I'll just follow you in the *Scylla.*"

Jack stops packing and locks eyes with me. "You wouldn't?"

"You could always join me since it's the only vessel that can submerge. They'll never see us coming. The inside is big enough for the both of us too. Be realistic, Jack. This is the only chance we both have to save everyone."

Jack pulls his shoulders back and his eyes narrow. "Marius doesn't want to be saved."

"That's the serum talking and you know it," I say.

"Sela, this is why I didn't tell you."

"I can still reach him."

"You're not focused," Jack says. "I'm going there to save Pearl and you're only going to slow me down."

"You're not going to save Pearl in this piece of junk." I jut a finger toward the tiny vessel.

"Fiiiine," he drawls out dramatically. "I'll take the *Scylla*. Alone."

"Not a chance."

Jack opens his mouth to say something but then looks at Una, Marin, and Ethan running for us down the dock.

Jack sighs. "Great, here comes the cavalry."

"You can't stop me!" I shout at Una.

Ethan and the others reach us at the boat slip and wait for Jack to say something.

"Help me move these to the *Scylla*," Jack says to Ethan. "I guess I'm not going alone after all."

Ethan claps a hand on Jack's back and then grabs a few weapons from the vessel.

"I'm going with you," Marin says, stepping closer to me.

Jack lets out a loud, exasperated sigh. "I didn't invite *any* of you!"

"No, you're not," Una snaps at Marin.

"Finally, some words of wisdom," Jack mutters under his breath.

"Shut up, Jack," I growl as he carts off next to Ethan with an armload of supplies.

"Who else is going to pilot the ship?" Marin asks.

"Not you." Una arches an eyebrow.

"I can do this," Marin insists. "She needs us."

"You're right," Una says. "That's why I'm going."

"What?" Marin and I say in unison.

Una turns to me. "I know I can't stop you, so I'm coming."

"No—"

"It has to be me," Una cuts me off.

I glance at Marin, but she doesn't argue.

"Neither of you are coming," I say. I can't lose any more of my Sisters. Derya's soft brown eyes flash in my mind.

"Sorry, I'm coming." Una grabs a metal box from the ground and marches across the dock toward the *Scylla*.

There's no fighting when Una is like this. She's the most stubborn person I know. Even more than Jack.

"I'm not fighting with you anymore," I say as I catch up to Una.

I glare at Jack, who is standing a few feet away. He has to see that all of this is fixable. Nerissa turned Marius into something terrible, and I'll find a way to bring him back.

He shakes his head but doesn't protest. He knows that he's lost this battle.

I swing my gaze back to Una. "I will get Marius back no matter what."

"That's why I'm coming," Una says.

I give her a weak smile.

When all of the supplies are moved to the *Scylla*, Ethan jumps through the ship's open hatch and makes his way in. I turn to Jack and he shrugs in defeat.

"More the merrier," he derides, rolling his eyes.

I heave a frustrated sigh. "Whatever, Jack."

Marin stands on the dock while the rest of us, plus Nyx, board the vessel.

"Marin?" I call out.

She shoots me a scowl.

"Inform everyone on Avalon to be on alert," I order.

"For what?" Marin asks.

"If Jack or I give the signal, you need to move Avalon to a new location, with or without us." It's hard to imagine since we've worked so hard to get Avalon functional again. But we need to protect the settlement from Nerissa.

Marin's eyes widen, but she nods, and the scowl falls from her face. She raises her hand and waves goodbye.

I return the gesture and head below deck to help Una prepare the vessel for departure. Neither of us speaks as we complete the protocols. The engine purrs to life.

Each of the crew sits in silence at a different station on the top deck. This is going to be a long trip.

On the ship's control screen, the glowing digital map hovers above the console. Our destination appears to be only a short distance away. But looks are deceiving. The journey will take several hours to reach the coordinates Marius had provided.

Una clicks her fingers over the screen and then turns the vessel on autopilot toward our destination. She shoves off her chair and walks over to me.

I wait to hear another reprimand.

"I need to tell you something." She stares at a small box in her hands.

I stare at the black container. "What's that?"

"I found something a few days ago." Una leans closer to me and whispers as if she doesn't want Jack to hear. But he's still off in his own world. "It's an antidote. For Marius."

I lean forward in my chair. "What? How?"

"We uncovered the information after accessing Nerissa's systems. I don't know why but it wasn't purged like most of the data. There must not have been time for a complete system wipe."

I push off my chair. "Why didn't you come to me right away? Who else knew?"

She opens the box, revealing serum hypospray. "We needed time to create the cure."

Heat rushes to the surface of my skin as I grab the box. "You still could have told me."

"There's more." She eyes Jack, who's staring at us now, of course. "If we don't use the serum on him in the next twenty-four hours, the antidote won't work. And beyond that, the serum might fail or worse. We won't be able to test effectiveness first."

"I can't believe you," I growl.

"I didn't want to get your hopes up," Una says. "I thought Marius was gone for good, and with the limited time frame—"

I slam the cover of the box closed.

"I wanted you to have peace of mind," she says. Her voice is soft and warm, but the sound only makes my skin heat up.

"You wanted to be in control," I say, shoving my shoulder into hers as I brush past her. Quickly, I shut the door to our sleeping quarters and lock it. I can't even look at her right now. I'm her captain. How dare she keep anything from me?

I lean my back against the wall of the cabin and slide my body to the floor. I clutch the box to my chest as if it's rare treasure. My heart speeds up with panic. I lower the box, unfasten the lock, and then open the lid, revealing the antidote inside.

What if Jack is right and the serum has progressed so far that Marius really doesn't want to be rescued? Will twenty-four hours be enough time to convince him.

CHAPTER 4

Jack

I PRESS MY hands against my thighs, trying to stop them from bouncing. I knew that it would take a while to get to Marius, and in turn, Pearl. But this is torture.

Nyx sits on one of the stations, completely still. Her eyes don't even flicker. Even she's bored.

Peering out of the *Scylla*'s curved front window doesn't help since it's completely dark. Clouds hide the light from the moon. So, we must rely on the radar instead.

Una's hands hover over the screens as if she's about to strike some invisible threat at any moment.

I'm about to stand up and pace the room release some pent-up energy when an alarm sounds overhead. The lights flicker on the top deck, and I spring from my chair.

I rush over to Ethan's station. "What's that?"

"We're approaching the destination," Una says, without taking her eyes off her station.

Nyx flickers to life and flits over to my shoulder.

"Submerge, now," I order.

I don't miss the look she gives me, but I promptly ignore it. I don't have time for her attitude. I'm running this mission; she's the tagalong.

"Do it."

Una obeys.

I grip the top of Ethan's chair as my stomach swoops with our descent. Marius's recording replays in my mind, and I hope this plan doesn't get Pearl killed. He said come alone, and I've done anything but.

"Give me an update," Sela's voice calls out from the other end of the room. She strides past me and settles next to her Sister. Then she places the small box I saw earlier onto the edge of the table, peering over Una's shoulder.

"We're close to the coordinates," Una says quickly, avoiding Sela's eyes.

In all the hours spent in close proximity, neither Sister has managed to resolve their issues. But, distracting myself with their drama isn't going to put Pearl back into my arms, either.

"Don't go any farther," I say.

Una and Sela whip their attention to me.

I clear my throat. "We need to do this right, and not just charge in there like a frenzy of sharks looking for a meal."

"He's right," Ethan says. "Marius isn't stupid. He probably knows or expects Jack won't come alone."

I clap a hand on his shoulder. At least someone on this vessel is on my side. "We still have the element of surprise. I doubt Marius would guess that I took the *Scylla*."

Sela shakes the red waves from her shoulders. "Alright, how should we do this?"

I know letting go of the reins is hard for Sela, but I appreciate her support. Getting to Pearl means getting to Marius. She's on board.

"We're at a safe depth," Una adds. "Out of sensor range."

Raking a hand through my hair, the plan forms in my mind. "Sela, you'll bring me to the surface. I'll meet with Marius, giving you time to infiltrate the *Echelon* and, hopefully, administer that hypospray."

Sela blinks, hard.

I shrug. "Ethan filled me in."

Una and Sela glance at each other.

"Ethan knew about it too," Una says.

Sela's lips mash into a thin white line, but I carry on. We're here, and I'm not going to waste any more time.

"Should we think about this some more?" Ethan asks. "Possibly a backup plan if something goes wrong?"

"Marius asked for me, so he knows I'm coming. We must move. Pearl needs me."

Nyx buzzes around my head, her eyes flickering green. She lands on my shoulder and leans against me.

"Ethan's right," Una pipes in.

"I agree," Sela says. "We need a backup."

I shake my head, hard enough that Nyx jumps off my shoulder. "The more time we sit here, the longer Pearl is in danger."

Una opens a drawer under her station. She pulls out a set of earbuds. "Wear these."

"Yes," Sela says, taking the comm.

"As long as you remain in close range to the *Scylla*, we can keep tabs on you," Una says. "If things go badly, we'll know."

Ethan looks to me for approval.

"OK." I swipe the other set from Una's palm.

"Let's suit up." Sela waves her hand for me to follow her.

In the corner of the room, several wetsuits hang on the wall. Sela picks a dark green suit from one of the hooks and hands it over.

"Really?" I tilt my head. "What is this? I don't do skin tight."

Sela scoffs. "Do you want your lungs to collapse? Just put on the compression suit and let's go."

I sigh and make my way to a partitioned dressing area and then strip down. I pull up the stretchy suit. It's surprisingly warm inside.

The suit Sela wears looks different than mine, sleeker. I suppose a girl who can swim underwater for hours doesn't need something so bulky. Her suit fits her like a glove while mine feels restrictive—um, down below.

"Please tell me this is a man's suit? Not everything is fitting!"

She rolls her eyes. "It will keep you alive; that's all you need to worry about."

Sela whips around and walks back to the bridge and over to Una's station. She grabs the small box of hypospray and tucks the package into a side pocket of her suit.

My body buzzes with nerves, and I need to get moving. I rub my hands over my torso, making sure the suit is on right. Complications before getting to the *Echelon* aren't an option.

"Ready?" I ask.

"As I'll ever be," Sela says.

Ethan and I bump fists. Nyx's eyes are still flashing, and I pat her on the head. "Don't worry about me. I'll be fine."

I turn to Sela. "Let's go."

Una calls out for Sela from behind, then mutters an apology.

Sela holds up a hand to stop her. "Save it for when we come back with Marius."

Sela slides past me, waving me from the bridge.

The compression chamber waits at the end of a short hallway. The ceiling is so low there's barely room for me to stand as we walk. The thick metal door is already open, revealing the cramped white room beyond. It's just big enough for the both of us.

The sizeable circular handle in the center of the door stares at me like one big glaring eye. I draw in a steeling breath. *I'm coming for you, Pearl.*

"This is yours too," Sela says, handing over a helmet the same color as my suit. I shove it on and, with a click on the back of my neck, Sela seals the helmet to my suit. It's a pretty fancy piece of tech. Several more pops tell me the seal is secure.

Her mouth quirks as she checks the seal a few times and, when she's finished, her green eyes meet mine. "You OK in there?"

Despite my thumping heart and the desire to rip the dang thing off again, I knock on the top of the helmet and give a thumbs-up.

Her hands are still on my shoulders, and I cock my head to the side, wondering what the holdup is. Before I can ask, she pulls me close to her. She knocks the breath out of me as she squeezes. But soon, she loosens and gives me a quick pat on the shoulder.

She's nervous, too.

"Ready?" she asks.

"As I'll ever be," I say through our connected comms.

"OK." She presses a switch, and the inner door closes.

The moment the lock *clicks*, the chamber floods with water. Sela grabs my hand, and I squeeze it tight. She's my buoy, and I have full faith that she will get me to the surface before the ocean flattens me like seaweed.

She faces the exterior door while I draw in big breaths. "Breathing slower helps."

"Says the girl with gills."

She twists my hand hard enough that it might hurt someone not enhanced like us.

I smirk, and my breathing slows.

When the water reaches my shoulders, the outer door opens, sucking us into the murky depths of the ocean.

The pressure of the water increases, compressing every inch of my body. Instinctively, I hold my breath, but I catch myself. I will my racing heart to slow down.

Sela wastes no time. I can barely see her through the darkness and bubbles. Good thing we're holding hands. I hope that Una was right and that Marius won't see us approach under cover of night, either.

Even though we travel hundreds of feet toward the surface, with Sela by my side, it doesn't take much time. She does most of the work. Still, water isn't my thing.

We emerge from the sea, and I immediately remove my helmet. It folds into pieces, nestling neatly into a compartment of my suit, right behind my neck.

Sela scans the distance.

"Well, that wasn't much fun," I say.

She splashes me, and the spray gets me in the eyes. I wipe away the droplets and grin.

"Sela?" Una says in my ear.

Sela presses her finger against her ear. "We're at the surface." She scowls and clicks off without saying anything else.

"OK," I say, not wanting to get involved with Sisterly drama. "I'm going to fly onto the ship's deck. Hopefully, Marius won't be able to resist an immediate meeting. I'll stall him long enough for you to go below and find a way in."

"Sounds good," she says and swims closer to me. "Ready for lift off?"

I nod, and then she dips below the surface. Bubbles ripple around me, and then, without any other warning, I'm popped out of the water. My ability takes over. I glide higher into the sky, peering out into the distance, before looking back down to see Sela watching me. For anyone else, the ocean would appear to go on for miles without anything in sight. But no one else has my engineered sight.

Along the horizon, the faint outline of the *Echelon* mocks me. Curling my lip, I take off toward the vessel.

A splash from below indicates that Sela is right behind me. She's close to the surface but, as we approach the vessel, her form disappears into the depths.

I hover far enough away that I should still be invisible to the ship, but I spot several armed goons patrolling the deck. At least ten weave around the canons, pacing every inch of the large ship like they're expecting me. Probably are.

I watch for a while, plotting the best place to land. I'm so close to Pearl that I can almost feel her presence.

I try to ignore my trembling hands and count to one hundred in my head instead.

Then, at ninety-nine, I shoot toward the boat, dropping onto the deck; only two of the thugs catch sight of me. I land and put my hands in the air. No need for unnecessary gunfire, especially in my direction.

A few men start shouting and then, before I can fully react, I'm surrounded. The guys are all gritted teeth and narrowed eyes. They move in closer to me, and one of their guns pokes me in the back.

"I'm surrendering." I wiggle my fingers. "I suggest you back off, or it won't be pretty."

"Keep your mouth shut, boy," one snarls.

"I was invited here. Surely your captain won't appreciate you treating his guest like a criminal. Get Captain Cook and Marius out here."

"I think you mean Captain Thacher," Marius says in a deep voice, strutting out onto the deck. "This is my operation now."

A few of the guards move aside, but their guns remain pointed at me. Cook trudges along behind Marius, clearly not thrilled by the mutiny, and maybe even regretting his choice to drag Marius off Avalon.

Marius passes under one of the lights hanging from the mast. He's dressed in a long, dark red overcoat, the color of blood. Reminds me of the last time I saw him.

I glance at his hand—or where his hand used to be— and a sharp straight blade slides out and points directly in my face. "We have some business to discuss."

CHAPTER 5

Jack

"WHAT DO YOU think of my newest enhancement, Flynn?" Marius asks.

"As long as you like it," I say, unable to take my eyes off the blade.

By the curl of his lip, I can tell he's on edge. Nerissa's injection makes him like this, volatile and unpredictable. I need to be smart.

"Marius, once again, I'm sorry about all that," I say to keep him calm.

His eyes fix on mine. "You're sorry?"

"Yeah, I am."

Marius tips his head in thought. "Sorry isn't going to bring back my hand."

He storms toward me. We're nose to nose, his teeth bared, and there's nothing left of the kid I knew. Now, I only see the effects of Nerissa's serum.

Gritting my teeth, I try to remain calm. I must, for Pearl's sake.

Someone behind me shifts and Marius' attention snaps to his crew. "I said don't move! That includes all of you. This business is between me and Flynn."

I don't dare look at the person who moved. All I can focus on is keeping his new blade-hand away from my body.

"Marius," I say in a low, calm tone. "I'm here now and have done everything you've asked. You can let Pearl go. She has nothing to do with this."

"Where is Sela?" Marius asks as if he didn't hear me. "I have no doubt she and her *Sisters*, or maybe even your own pathetic crew, are nearby. Not that it matters. I'm more than capable of taking all of you down."

"I have no idea," I say flatly. "I came alone as you asked."

Marius puffs out a breath and a smile spreads across his lips. "Well, either way, you're here. We have business to deal with. It's simple: if you win, Flynn, then I promise to let Pearl go."

I can take Marius down. He's reckless and battling whatever the injection is doing to his head. I can use that to my advantage. If this is what I need to do to free Pearl, then so be it.

My heart begins to race and a flashing image of Sela's face pops into my mind. As much as I want to get Pearl back, I need to think of my friend too. Sela will be devastated. There must be another way.

I sigh. "We found a cure for what Nerissa did to you. We don't have to do this."

"A cure? For what? I feel better than ever thanks to that Witch."

"Maybe you should think about it," Cook suggests in a near whisper.

Marius turns to his old friend.

With a shaky hand, Cook pushes his glasses higher up the bridge of his nose. "C-Captain," he sputters.

Marius cocks his head to the side. "Why would I think about a cure when I can do this?"

Marius's hand flies out and backhands Cook. Cook's green eyes roll back into his head, and he crumples to the ground.

A breath catches in my throat. I don't dare move, but I stare at the body on the ground, willing him to get up. Even though Cook isn't conscious, the steady movement of his chest forces a tight breath from my lungs. He's alive. Knocked out, but alive.

Marius needs to be stopped. He's gone out of his mind.

Sorry, Sela.

I take what might be my only chance and lunge at him. My legs move forward, but something clasps around my neck and chokes off my next breath.

I whip around and come face to chest with stone-faced Watts as he moves his hands off the collar. His bulging muscles flex, daring me to do something.

Not again with this thing! I recognize the restraint tech from the one Nerissa saddled me with. But this time, it's locked on my throat instead of my waist.

Throwing my fists out, they land on Watts broad chest and he rockets backward, crashing hard into the bow of the boat.

OK, I still have my strength. Maybe Watts hadn't turned the device on yet. I reach up, expecting to shoot off into the air, but nothing happens.

Crap.

"There's no retreat," Marius scoffs, and gestures for the other men to back away from us. "No one interferes, got it?"

The men mutter their agreement, but they're still armed and ready for whatever is about to happen.

Marius's teeth flash. "We finish this, now."

Before I can blink, Marius is in front of me swinging. I barely dodge his fist. He's fast. His strikes are all over the place, keeping me on my toes as I slide across the deck. I try to back away from him, but he's nearly on top of me the whole time. Holding my arms up, I block several hard hits. I avoid his blade as the sharp edge nearly cuts my chest. My forearms burn from his heavy attacks.

My best move is flight, and he knows that, so this fight is hardly fair.

Marius's nostrils flare. "Fight me! Don't you want to save your *precious* Pearl?"

I hate her name on his lips. Swiping my leg out, I connect with his shin. He stumbles but catches himself.

The momentary distraction gives me only a second to flee or fight. Since I can't escape very far with this thing around my neck, I choose to fight. It's my only chance to save her.

As Marius straightens, I hook him in the jaw with my fist. Pain explodes in my hand, but I ignore the agony. Guess the upgrades he got are pretty intense.

Marius lets out a guttural roar, a sound so inhuman it causes a chill to run down my spine. I block his first blow with my arm and then lean in close to him. Too close.

Before I can correct myself, Marius's fist lands squarely on my nose with a sickening crunch. My eyes close, blanketing the world in darkness. Warm blood trickles down my throat, and I gag on the metallic taste.

I backpedal blindly.

When I open my eyes, the world is blurry, but Marius's red coat is a beacon in the darkness. The blade where his hand should be shoots out in front of him and a searing heat slices across my midsection.

Doubling over, my knees slam into the deck. Sucking in a breath, I try to recover, but my body has other ideas.

Marius laughs, and the hairs on my arms prickle at the wicked sound. I move my hand away from my stomach and a thick line of blood trails across my arm. His black boots stop in front of me, and I stare at them trying to keep conscious. Between him smashing my nose and digging his blade into me, I have to be losing a lot of blood. And fast.

Marius kneels in front of me. His blade presses against my neck and I hold my breath. He puts enough pressure to force me to lift my chin.

"It looks like Pearl will see you after all," Marius says with a look of sadistic pleasure. "But you won't be alive to gaze into her devastated eyes."

Never.

Gritting my teeth, I summon whatever strength is still inside of me and push it all at Marius. He underestimates me by being so close. My palms connect with his chest, and he launches backward, slamming into the edge of the ship.

Still unable to fly, I spring up. Black stars fill my vision as my injured body tries to slow me down. But I won't die before seeing Pearl again.

Marius grunts and reaches for the back of his head. He doesn't get up.

Behind me, the clomp of boots make their way toward us.

"The captain said not to interfere," Cook growls.

I nod at the old man and step closer to Marius. My shirt is soaked with blood, and I continue to swallow what feels like buckets of the thick liquid.

I can finish him with one blow. Marius was stupid not to restrain all my strength. His eyes lock with mine, and he attempts to scramble up. I drive my foot into his chest, pushing him down again with a thud.

I ball my hand into a fist. Marius has control over his crew, so I'm the only one who can stop him. I kneel beside him and wrap my hands around his neck. Now he knows what this stupid restraint feels like. I squeeze my hands and Marius starts to choke.

"Jack, stop!" Sela calls out from behind me.

She dashes to my side and drops down next to us. With shaking hands, she presses the hypospray into his exposed neck.

Marius's eyes close, and his entire body slackens. His mouth hangs open. And if I squint, he looks asleep.

Still, I don't release my grip around his neck. This guy just tried to kill me.

"It's over," Sela says, clawing at my hands.

I don't let go.

"Jack, let him go!" Sela shouts, but I don't move. I can't. Marius and his family have put me through too much. Ending him will end everything.

"Jack, Marius is our friend," Sela says, her voice peppered with fear. "This was all Nerissa. Let him go. She hurt him just as much as she hurt us. Let him go so we can find Pearl."

Pearl.

The sound of her name snaps me back.

I release Marius and launch up from the ground. I immediately regret standing as the ship tilts at a weird angle.

Sela grabs my arm, and I wince, falling toward her and letting my friend support some of my weight. Everything hurts, but the battle is far from over.

The crew of the *Echelon* stare at me with mixed emotions, but mostly hatred. Snarls and frowns fill their faces. I nearly killed their captain. Cook shuffles between the crew, Sela, and me.

"This isn't going to end well for any of us," I say. "You all need to back off."

The men look at each other for confirmation. Sela and I could take down most of them, but we won't win. Not in my condition.

"Stand down," Cook shouts. His voice holds the authority of a captain, and the crew immediately falls into rank.

My legs give out from under me, and I take Sela down with me in a heap.

She scrambles to sit up. Her eyes widen as she takes in the blood on my dark suit. "What happened?"

"Marius has a new hand. When I say hand, I mean a shiny new weapon that slices and dices."

Sela glances at Marius, who is still passed out and pulls up the fabric of my suit from the tear. I wince from the sting.

"I'll be back with some supplies," Cook says and leaves us.

"Don't move," Sela says, stroking my hair. "It will be OK. Everything will be OK."

"Do you ever stop being so positive? It's sickening, you know."

She smiles, only a small one. But that gives me a little hope that I'll leave this ship in one piece.

"Jack!" Pearl's voice rips through the air.

She stumbles out of one of the doorways. Her thick, dark hair falls over her face as she drops to the deck. But when her eyes meet mine, my entire world shifts, the blackness pushes out to my periphery, and all I see is her.

61

CHAPTER 6

Sela

"ARE YOU OK?" Jack asks Pearl. His hands touch every feature on her face, and he brings her close for a tight embrace.

"Yes," Pearl says. "I was so worried about you!"

"Me? You're all I've thought about. Every single day."

There's a deck filled with crew members and these two are acting as if they're the only two people on the planet.

So much of me wants to be happy Jack found Pearl but, instead, my heart sinks in my chest. Marius rests peacefully on the deck in front of me. Even though the "cure" knocked him out, I have no idea if the serum worked. My gaze wanders to his missing hand and I cringe. The blade has retracted, and nothing but a metal device sits where his hand should be. Marius's blood slides down the metal sides and soaks his coat sleeve.

When he wakes up, I want to be the first person he sees.

Loud footfalls clomp across the deck. I turn to find six men, including Cook, walk toward us, their eyes fixed on Marius.

I jump up to meet them. I know Cook liked Marius growing up, but he's the kind of guy who mostly looks out for himself. And I have no idea what his intentions are at this point. I throw my arms out at my sides and stand between them and Marius. "I gave him a cure. He's not a threat—"

Cook puts up his hands. "Sela, I'm only here to check on him. We're on your side."

My chest hitches and my vision blurs with tears. I have no idea if that's true but, right now, my choices are limited. I step aside.

Cook's jaw tenses and he kneels at Marius's side. "You poor boy." He places his hand on Marius's forehead. "He hasn't been himself since Avalon. I've tried as best as I could. I hope your cure works."

I glance up at the mob now hovering behind Cook. "Are you sure your crew feels the same way?"

The tense looks on most of their faces make the fact Marius didn't make the best captain in his prior state pretty obvious. If his anger at Jack was any indication, I doubt he treated them very well.

Cook motions to his crew. "There will be no more fighting on this vessel tonight."

They ease back, but I'm still not sure I like the tension remaining among the group.

A loud grunt sounds from the other side of the deck. I whip my head around. A massive Watts shakes his head a few times and then wanders over toward us. He wobbles on his feet and grabs one of the crew members before nearly smacking to his knees on the cold, hard deck.

"What about him?"

Cook chuckles and shakes his head. "Watts is loyal. He won't be a problem for your lot."

It takes several of the men to help Watts to his feet as they lead him below deck. I have no idea what happened before I arrived, but either Marius or Jack did a number on him.

"Get Marius to the med bay," Cook barks at the two nearby crew members.

I rise and give them the space they need. The two crewmates heft Marius up between them and then follow Cook across the deck.

"I'm coming with you," I insist.

Cook gestures for me to follow. I obey, glancing back at Jack.

Pearl's hands move across Jack's stomach. There's a slash across his compression suit that's wet with blood.

"Go, I'm fine. My nanos are already healing me." Jack says, even though he winces at Pearl's touch.

Turning away, I leave Jack to heal on his own. It's a good thing Marius didn't slash Jack any deeper or else Jack would be in the med bay too.

I navigate the long hallway below deck, following Cook's echoing voice as he directs his crew where to place Marius. Just as I arrive, the two crew members exit the med bay. I rush inside as if I'm tethered to Marius by an invisible rope.

"You can sit," the medic says to me from across the room. He's a short, thin man with a scraggly black beard. His eyes bug out of his head, but his crooked smile is friendly enough.

I sit on a small metal chair next to the bed, and I take Marius's hand while the man examines him. A million questions whiz around in my head as he runs a scanner over Marius's body, but I hold off asking.

"All his vitals are improving, and his stress chemicals are moving back into a normal range," the medic says to Cook and me before checking Marius's restraints. "Now we wait for him to come to and see if any of the effects are lasting."

I look to Cook.

"He's going to be fine," Cook says, walking to the other side of the room. He leans against the wall, crossing his arms in front of his chest. "We'll make sure."

Marius's chest rises and falls in a steady rhythm, lulling me into a near trance until something snaps in my ear.

"Sela!" Una calls into my comm. "Are you OK?"

I wince and press the comm. "I'm fine. Everything is good."

"Your comm was out for a bit," Una says.

I roll my eyes. "I needed to turn it off."

Una sighs. "We're coming up."

I'd rather them not. But whatever. If not for Una, I wouldn't have had the cure. "OK," I say and relay the message to Cook.

"I'll inform the others. Now excuse me while I check the status of the ship and crew," Cook says. "Notify me when Marius is awake."

"I will," I say. "Thank you for everything."

Cook nods. "Let's give them some privacy." He waves at the medic, and they leave the room.

Part of me wants Cook to stay since I have no guarantee Marius will wake up in a logical state. But the rest of me only wants us to be alone. Stroking his hand, I try to will consciousness back into him.

I study our hands and the stark contrast between our skin colors; Marius's is brown and mine is pale with a pink tinge. Taking a shaky breath, I try to calm the churning of my stomach.

Bringing his hand up to my lips, I gently kiss his fingers. "Please, wake up," I choke out.

Marius's fingers twitch, and I spring up from the chair. His eyes roll around under his eyelids, and his mouth opens and closes, even though nothing comes out.

I squeeze his hand. "Marius, it's me, Sela."

"Sela?" he croaks.

"Yes." Excitement wells in my chest. "You're safe."

His eyelids flutter open, and he blinks a few times as if he's having trouble focusing. I glance at the door. Should I get Cook or the medic to take a look at him?

Marius's hand slips away from mine as he pushes his fist into the cot and sits up straighter.

"How do you feel?" I ask.

He scratches his chin, and his eyes meet mine. "I—" his breathing intensifies, and he stares forward, his eyes darting back and forth. He winces and then swallows a few times.

"Flynn," Marius says. "I—" he holds up the new enhancement where his hand should be. Looking it over like he's never seen the attached blade before.

"He's fine."

Marius shakes his head furiously and shifts as if he's trying to get up.

I rest my hand on his to settle him. "You need to rest. Don't rush to get up."

"Sela." His voice is thick with emotion. He rubs his hand over his face. "I don't know what came over me."

"What do you remember?"

His face scrunches up in confusion. "Not much. Mostly flashes and blurs."

"None of this was your fault. Nerissa did this to you. After everything that happened with your father—"

"My dad? He's—"

"He's gone, Marius."

Marius's shoulders slump, and he sits back against the wall behind him. His chin almost touches his chest. "I remember now. It wasn't Jack's fault. Thacher's death is no one's fault except for Nerissa's."

Marius's body has relaxed there is no rage against Jack. It gives me hope that the cure worked, but I want to be sure. "How do you feel right now?"

Marius thinks for a moment as if he's considering his state of mind. "Like I got hit by a whale . . . but I feel less like a monster." He sighs and then lifts his gaze to mine. "Thank you."

He draws me into his arms. I melt against him, and the warm feeling of safety moves through me. Marius is back.

His breathing is shaky, but understandable after all he's been through.

Voices and footsteps echo down the hallway and I pop up from Marius's arms just in time for Jack and Pearl to walk into the room. When Jack sees Marius, he stops in his tracks.

Marius shifts on the cot.

Pearl's eyes widen. "I was hoping the medic would look at Jack's wound . . ." her voice trails off as the two guys continue to stare at each other.

Apparently, they didn't expect Marius to be awake.

"Sit over here," Pearl says, pulling Jack across the room toward an empty chair. She plops him into the chair while she applies pressure to his wound.

There has to be something to break the thick cloud of tension in the room. I squeeze Marius's leg, shove off the cot, and then cross to the opposite end of the room.

"I'm Sela," I say, extending a hand to Pearl.

She smiles and shakes my hand. "I know." She tucks a tendril of her hair behind her ear. "Jack has told me about you before."

I tilt my head and look at Jack. "You have?"

Jack rolls his eyes. "Don't think about it too much."

"Considering we weren't on such good terms for a while, I hope he didn't say anything too terrible."

Pearl tips her head to the side and her lips turn up into a sweet smile. "Jack never said a negative thing about you."

"Alright, enough of that," Jack says, and then lowers his voice, "How's Thacher?"

"Um . . . I'm right here . . . and I'm fine," Marius says. "You knocked me around pretty good . . . twice."

The corner of Marius's mouth lifts, and I wait for Jack to respond. He doesn't.

Finally, Marius clears his throat. "Are you OK, Flynn?"

"Yeah. Fine," Jack grits out through clenched teeth. "Sorry I took your hand."

Marius holds out his arm, studying the metal contraption. But I know the tension is more than the missing hand. Jack shot Marius's dad.

"We both have regrets." Marius grunts as he swings his legs off the cot.

"Are you sure you want to do that?" I ask him.

"Yes," Marius says through gritted teeth.

"Maybe you should rest a little while longer," I say.

"No," Marius insists. "I need to do this."

I move closer, fully expecting him to topple over at any moment. But instead, he flexes his hand and grasps his bicep. "I feel good, still strong actually. Really strong."

"Welcome to the freak club," Jack quips. "We'll print out your membership card in a few."

Marius's eyes widen.

"Don't mind him," I say. "We have no idea if the effect is permanent or not. Right now, I'm just happy you're standing on your own."

Marius tosses a smile my way.

A blaring alarm rips through the air, and I immediately cover my ears. The lights in the room flash and several crew members run past the med bay door.

I glance at Jack.

"Go," Jack says.

Marius and I rush out of the room and sprint up the stairs toward the main deck.

"What's going on?" Marius asks, but none of the crew responds.

I scan the deck and finally spot Cook in conversation with a few men on the bridge. I grab for Marius's hand and pull him through the distracted crew members. Cook doesn't notice our arrival as he's barking orders to the crew members below.

Marius releases my hand and walks up behind Cook. He pauses for a second before he plops his hand onto Cook's shoulder.

Cook turns around, and his eyes flash when he sees Marius. "Captain?"

Marius bows his head slightly. "No, I think I'm leaving that job up to you for now."

Cook clasps his shoulder and brings Marius closer to him. "There's something on the bow of that boat."

"Captain," one of the crew members says, pointing to a display screen. The image is fuzzy, but as the crew member adjusts the digital scope, the object sharpens.

A monstrous, scaly beast stands on the small boat's bow. Its shoulders rise and fall quickly as if it's hyperventilating. Its mouth is open, revealing massive sharp teeth, nearly matching the length of the claws on its fingers. I've never seen a creature like this before. Possibly a remnant of Nerissa's experiments.

"What *is* that?" Marius asks.

Cook's bushy eyebrows mash together. "I have no idea, but the beast looks angry."

CHAPTER 7

Sela

MY EYES ARE glued to the display screen as the terrifying creature continues to stare off into the distance. It's not quite looking our way, but it's only a matter of time.

Marius shifts next to me and wraps his arm around my waist.

"What do we do about that thing?" Its very presence sends a shiver down my spine.

"Captain?" Marius asks Cook.

Cook shakes his head as if clearing his thoughts. "It's not doing anything right now. There's no use approaching the creature until it makes the first move."

It's a good thing it's far off in the distance, not close enough to attack us or whatever the beast plans on doing. I feel bad for any other ship out there—

"Una!" I cry. She's bringing the *Scylla* to the surface. Marius and Cook flick their attention my way.

I flip on my comm device. "Una, are you there?"

"Yes," Una says. Her voice forces a relieved breath from my lungs. "We've just broken the surface and are on our way to you."

"No!" I say, snapping my fingers at the crew member. I wave at the digital scope. I need to see where Una is in relation to that *thing.*

He looks to Cook, who nods his head in agreement.

"There's a monstrous creature nearby," I say to Una. "It's big, ugly, and looks pretty angry. You need to dive. Now!"

I swivel the scope until I spot the *Scylla* in the distance. The ship is closer to the creature than we are. Glancing out the front bridge window, the outline of the *Scylla* appears in full view. That thing would be blind not to see the ship.

"What if I took a closer look?" Una asks. "If I take the *Scylla* under, I'll be able to see it without detection."

"No, I want you to retreat."

"We'll be fine," Una says. "And I can report the information back to you."

I chew on my lip. The sooner we get that creature away from the *Echelon,* the better. But we need to know what we're up against.

"Fine, but if that creature dives, you get out of there."

"Understood." The line cuts out.

Running a shaky hand through my hair, I watch as the *Scylla* descends. "She's going to get a closer look."

"Who is? Una?" Marius asks.

Moving the scope, I focus on the creature again. Its chin lifts, and then it whips its head to the side before diving into the water.

I'm unable to look away from the screen, gripping the scope hard enough to spasm the muscles in my hand.

"Where did it go?" Marius asks.

"Where do you think?" I press my comm. "Una! Abort mission."

There's utter silence on the line.

"We need to move the *Echelon* closer to help," Marius says.

Cook pushes his glasses farther up his nose. "Engaging that creature might not be the best idea."

"We're all aware of that," I say. "But we can't just sit here and watch that thing go after the *Scylla*."

Cook glances over at me and then back to the window.

"Engage the ship," he orders the crew member standing next to him. The man nods and walks over to the controls.

The *Scylla* is a sturdy vessel. Una knows how to pilot the ship away from that thing.

I hope.

The *Echelon* lurches, and Marius grabs my arm to steady me. It doesn't take long for this large ship to get up to speed. In my mind, I close the distance between us and the creature's small vessel. My heartbeat thunders in my ears. Una will get out of there if she senses danger. Maybe she'll lead the creature away until she can circle back to us.

A flurry of bubbles rustles the surface of the ocean as the *Scylla* ascends. Water rushes down the ship's smooth, rounded hull. But when the water recedes thick, black smoke billows from the top hull. The haze eventually clears and terror squeezes the air from my lungs. The creature grips the top of the *Scylla* with one hand, his claws from the other digging into the hull over and over.

Before I know it, I'm halfway to the edge of the *Echelon*. I won't let anything happen to Una or Ethan. I can't.

"Sela!" Marius calls.

I wave him off without turning. If I see Marius, I might not leave. "I have to save her."

"Don't be stupid!" he shouts and catches up to me just as I'm about to dive over the edge.

Whirling around, I shove my hands out, connecting with his hard chest. "I'm the only one who can get there in time."

"We need to think about this." Marius raises his hands high, ready to jump in after me. "You don't know what that creature can do. He's ripping apart a ship with his bare hands. I can't imagine what he'll do to you."

Peering out over the water, I see the *Echelon* is closing in on the damaged *Scylla* without slowing.

"Looks like Cook is planning on using every force necessary to get that thing. Just give him the opportunity before you get yourself killed."

I can barely swallow as my throat clenches. Leaving Una out there, defenseless, is killing me inside. I draw in a breath and wait for Cook to fire at the creature. But it doesn't happen.

My muscles twitch as my mind anchors me in place. I count the seconds in my head. We're close enough that a strike would knock the creature off the vessel. Then I could get to Una.

But before anything happens, the creature lifts its head and stares straight at us. A breath catches in my throat as I sense its intention before it acts.

The creature dives into the water and, in seconds, a silhouette ripples near the surface, coming straight for us. I glance at the *Scylla* and then to a wide-eyed Marius. His now clammy hand grips my arm with his new strength.

We stagger back a few steps before a wave of water crashes into the side of the *Echelon*. I yelp as the beast launches out of the water and lands right in front of us. The weight of the mutant's body reverberates over the deck of the vessel, and the vibrations travel up my legs.

Its dark eyes fall on us. No use being a hero today. Marius and I take off.

"Son," the beast says, as clear as day.

Marius stops in his tracks, and I nearly trip over his feet. He slowly circles to face the creature.

"What?" Marius mutters.

I seize Marius's arm and pull, but he's so much stronger than me now that yanking away is pointless.

Instead, Marius shakes me off and walks toward the creature.

I gawk at its giant claws, big enough to take Marius down with a flick of its wrist.

"Dad?" Marius whispers, getting closer still.

My mouth falls open as new horror surges through me. Jack killed Marius's father. I saw him die. The beast's heaving shoulders drop as Marius approaches, and something in its reptile eyes shifts, becoming more human.

"Marius, stop," I command. "We don't know—"

"I do!" Marius growls. A mix of anger and sadness flashes in his eyes.

Shouting voices and footsteps thunder over the deck. A dozen of Cook's men surround us, raising their weapons toward the intruder.

Marius turns toward them, lifting his arms up. "Stop. Don't attack. He's—" his voice barely reaches them as one of the crew member's fires at the beast, neutralizing Marius's pleas.

I duck down, covering my head from the rain of plasma and bullets.

Marius rushes forward, trying to plead with them as more gunshots fire. The bullets either miss or ricochet off the creature. Bursts of hot plasma have no effect on him either. It lets out a guttural roar and charges at the men.

A sickening *crack* fills my ears before a body sails in the air and overboard. I turn toward one of the screaming men. The place where his arm should be is now a gaping red hole. Seconds later, he's lifted into the air by his throat and then tossed overboard too.

The creature gouges its claws into another man's neck before hurling him across the deck. The lifeless body lands on the railing before sliding down into the watery depths below.

The beast roars again and spins around to face us. "You will all die!"

Shock ripples over the rest of the crew and they all turn and run.

"Dad, stop! You can't do this!" Marius calls to the creature as it stalks toward us.

Marius opens his arms in front of him, keeping me behind him.

"We can't stay." Every animal instinct is screaming for me to run, just like the crew. "It's going to rip us to shreds."

"No," Marius says. "Not yet."

The beast grunts, not stopping. We shuffle backward, trying to stay as far away from him as possible. But it's pushing us to the edge of the ship, cornering us. I could jump, but no way Marius can outswim this thing with one hand.

"It's not listening," I plead.

The beast lunges at us, showing off two rows of sharp teeth, saliva streaming from its mouth.

Marius wrestles for the beast's arms and grunts as his new strength keeps those claws from getting close to us. The blade on Marius's arm digs into the wrist of the creature, but it hardly flinches.

"Please—" Marius says through gritted teeth.

But any sliver of humanity I saw a moment ago is now gone. The beast clamps its mouth shut, lowers its head, and charges Marius. Within a heart-pounding second, Marius avoids the attack as the beast nearly slides into the railing before catching itself.

Barely thinking, I take a few steps toward it, but Marius throws out his arm to block my move

"Stop, Sela!" Marius turns to me and the beast grabs his shoulders.

With one sharp movement, the beast pins Marius to the ground. Even Marius's newfound strength is nothing compared to the scaly creature's. Their faces are close together. I can't breathe. I can't scream. Then the fearsome monster lets out what sounds like a laugh. A sound that ignites me into action.

I jump toward the brute, and its fist crashes into my stomach. All the air is knocked out of my lungs as I land against the ship's railing with a smack. A surge of pain radiates up and down my spine. I crumple onto the deck.

The beast lunges at Marius. I try to stand, but searing pain in my back prevents me.

"Sela?" Jack calls from behind me. "Are you—"

"Stay back!" I shout. Jack could enrage the beast even further.

As usual, he doesn't listen. Jack staggers out from below deck. His eyebrows mash together as he takes in the scene. Lifting off from the ground, he shoots toward us.

As if the monster has eyes in the back of its head, it shifts around and reaches toward Jack. He swoops away from its hand, barely avoiding the razor-sharp claws.

Marius twists away from under the beast and grabs its arms again, trying to restrain the creature. They grapple for several agonizing seconds before Marius tears away from its grasp.

I push off the ground and scan the air for Jack. He's gone.

The infuriated creature faces the other direction. I race for it. I gather all my strength and sweep my leg along the deck, making contact with its shin.

It staggers back, giving Marius a reprieve, but only for a second. It doesn't even give me another glance. It apparently only has eyes for Marius.

I try again, but its claws come inches from ripping me in two. The monster roars in Marius's direction.

From behind, a sharp whistle sounds and I swing toward the source. Jack is back, leaning heavily against the doorway, wincing in agony. Something sails through the air toward me.

Instinctively, I raise my hands and the box of hypospray from inside the ship lands in my palms.

Will the cure work on Marius's father? If this thing is even him?

Jack shrugs as if reading my thoughts.

But I must try. Or Marius is going to die. We all will.

I press my toes into the deck, not wanting to make a sound as I approach. Who knows how many tries I have before something worse happens.

The monster rounds toward me, and I race to the side, keeping out of his eye line. I grab one of the hyposprays and ready the serum. Marius throws the reptile to the deck.

With him distracted again, I take my chance. Leaping up from the ground, I land on his back, and slam the hypospray against the beast's neck, in between the scales. He pitches, and I wrench my arm around his neck to stay steady while injecting the cure.

The mutant reaches its hands up, and the claws almost cut into me. I slide off its back before it can sink its razor-sharp points into my flesh.

The creature cups its neck with one hand, where I injected the serum, while still gripping Marius with the other. The beast's thin lips draw back, baring rows of teeth, as Marius tries to wriggle away. The beast moves toward Marius, but then loses its balance and crashes against the deck.

In a last-ditch effort, it reaches for Marius, but he's too far away. The beast makes several attempts to stand up again and loses every time.

My heart rate begins to slow when the monster falls to the deck, face-first with a thud. And doesn't get up again.

Marius stares at the creature, drawing in gulps of air. Splotches of blood dot his shirt. But he's alive.

Cook, Watts, and several other crew members rush onto the deck with their weapons drawn.

Too little, too late, boys.

Marius once again wedges himself between Cook's crew and the beast.

"He's down. Don't hurt him." Marius glances over his shoulder. "It's my dad."

CHAPTER 8

Jack

THE MED BAY is packed with people while the oversized human-crocodile thing rests. Its huge limbs barely fit onto a bed with the rest of its body.

Marius is closest to the bed, holding hands with Sela. At least she's keeping some distance, though. Marius's head bows toward what used to be his father.

After the battle on the deck, I wonder if Marius is missing a screw in his head. There's no guarantee that the hypospray will work on the beast. As for me, I'm keeping my spot with Pearl next to the door for a quick getaway. Cook is smart and keeps to the back of the room too.

Marius glances over his shoulder and stares at me. I stare right back. If he's looking for a comforting friend, he's not going to find one. He has Sela for that.

"Can we go now?" I ask Pearl.

"You need to stay right here." She glares at me. "These are your friends and they need you."

Some friends. Three people in here have wanted to kill me at one point or another. Well, all save Sela.

Pearl pulls my arm away and inspects the wound across my stomach. I'm not worried. It's almost healed, and we have a bigger problem sitting right in front of us.

"You should take it easy," she says. "It's still red from flying."

I smile. She's the warmest girl I know. Seems fitting that she would worry about me, even though I'm enhanced. I think that's one of the reasons I love her so much.

Pearl brushes a stray hair off my forehead, and I melt into her touch. Locking eyes with her, I wrap my arm around her shoulder and pull her close to me. Inhaling the scent of her hair, my mind drifts to how lucky we were to find her.

"How *did* Marius find you?" I ask.

She flicks a glance at Marius and Sela, but they're having their own conversation.

"In all the chaos, I was able to get free from my secured quarters. Once I made it on deck, I knew it had to be your doing and I went to look for you. But Marius and Cook found me first. Marius's arm was gushing blood, so I asked if they needed help. I didn't even really know who he was, but he must have recognized me.

"I asked if he had seen you," she quietly continues. "He told me that you were on the *Echelon* and that, if I would help him onto the boat to get his wound cleaned and covered, he would take me to you." She nibbles the inside of her lip. "I wanted to see you so badly that I didn't notice the hate in his eyes until it was too late."

I push down my anger, reminding myself that Marius wasn't in control of his mind then. "You couldn't have known." If the opposite had happened, I would have followed Nerissa herself to find Pearl.

"We need to finish Nerissa," Sela says to Marius and Cook, interrupting my and Pearl's conversation.

She's right. Sela's the only person other than me who wants, more than anything, to see that Witch go down.

Sela's plan revolves around waiting for the crocodile to wake up from his slumber, so I basically zone out.

"I have some information," Pearl says. Her voice is so low that, at first, I think I had imagined it.

"What?" I ask.

"I have something to say," she says a little louder.

This time the others turn around. Cook's thick eyebrows squeeze together before releasing.

Sela's head tilts to the side. "What?"

Pearl glances at Marius and then back to her hands. "On Avalon, some of Nerissa's officers were a little loose with information sometimes. Not long before you and Jack came, I heard them discussing her plans to commandeer

Atlantis as their new base of operations. Sort of like a backup plan to Avalon."

Sela charges forward and stops in front of Pearl. "Are you sure you heard them say Atlantis?"

Pearl tosses a look at me and then nods. "Yes."

Sela's face falls. "My father. First, she gets away from us and now this?"

Pearl blinks. "Your father is in Atlantis?"

"Her father is Killian Tritus, founder of Atlantis," I say.

"Oh," she says, turning her gaze down.

Sela pinches her lips together and paces. "They made a deal. I can't go there."

"Why?" Pearl asks.

Sela stops. "Nerissa and my father worked out something years ago. He would stay out of things and she would keep her forces away. This goes against everything—I can't believe this. I have to warn him."

"We should start a course toward Atlantis." Marius comes to Sela's side. "There has to be something we can do. Nerissa sent my father here, probably hoping he would defeat us. She might be taking her time."

Cook nods. "I'm always up to visit new trade partners. I'll set the course."

"Let's not rush into this," I say.

Sela narrows her eyes. "If Nerissa is going to Atlantis, it's the next logical step for us."

I take a deep breath and glance at Pearl. As much as I want to exact revenge on Nerissa, I just found Pearl. She's safe with me. If we go to Atlantis, there are infinite possibilities for her to get hurt or taken again.

The rest of the group eyes me as if I'm the deciding vote on this plan. Sela is strong-willed; she'll go either way. But we're stronger together.

"I'm going," Pearl says.

Of course, she would say that. My chest tightens, but there's no way I can tell the group that I'm scared for my girlfriend's life and, therefore, we're staying put. I'll just look like a jerk. Then Cook, always on Marius's side, will boot me off the boat, since I'm not a part of the team. *And* Sela will never let me forget.

"Well, let's do this already," I say. "Might as well swim with the fishies."

CHAPTER 9

Sela

WE STAND on the bridge, looking out over the vast blue sea. The sun cuts through the horizon, shining down a small sliver of light in the distance. My stomach swirls with apprehension over my return to Atlantis. The broken *Scylla* bobs in the water, destroyed. We all almost died by Marius's father's hands, and I shudder.

Marius touches my arm, but I can't look at him yet. He'll see what I'm feeling, and I'm not sure if I'm ready to talk.

Una and Ethan are safe, but the sooner we get to Atlantis, the better. More than anyone else here, Una will understand why I'm not jumping for the opportunity to get back to our home. She grew up there too.

But I'm the one who pushed to get Nerissa and exact our revenge. With Pearl's information, the only way forward is to go back.

Glancing next to me, I feel a stab of jealousy. Pearl and Jack look as serene as anyone possibly could after everything. If we were going anywhere else, Marius and I might look the same.

"We can't travel on the *Echelon*." Cook interrupts my thoughts. "It can only take us so far. We need a submersible vessel."

I sigh, knowing what he's thinking. "The only way we can get to Atlantis is with a fully functional *Scylla*."

"Too bad Elijah didn't come with us," Jack says, quirking his lips. "There's not enough time to go back to Avalon and get him to do the repairs."

I shake my head. "It's out of the question." If Nerissa is heading to Atlantis, then I want to get there as soon as possible.

She might already be there though. Goosebumps ripple up my arms, and I try to rub them away.

Jack scratches his head. "So, who's here that can repair your submersible?"

"Me," a gruff voice says from behind us. A battered Watts approaches us. He flexes his hands, his eyes shooting daggers at Jack as if he's prepping for another fight. He cracks his knuckles and I cringe from the sound. Last time I saw him, he was carried below deck after his altercation with Jack. "I'm not sure if I should be helping any of you, though."

"Please," I say.

He brings his hand to his chin and rubs it as if thinking. "I suppose a little trade might be in order."

"A trade?" Jack asks, suspicious as ever.

Watts glances at his captain and the two share a weighted look. They planned this whole thing.

I narrow my eyes. Once a pirate, always a pirate.

Watts' lips quirk into a wicked grin and I'm one hundred percent positive this isn't going to be in our favor at all. "I'll help fix your ship if Captain Cook and I come with you all to Atlantis."

I scoff. "What? No way."

Watts crosses his arms and gives Jack a look, daring him to refuse. Jack and Marius look to me for the answer. This is my choice. It's my home. And inviting these two is a bad idea. Cook has been accommodating enough, but he also tried to double cross us on Avalon. If selling us out to Nerissa benefits him, he will. And I trust Watts about as far as I can throw him.

Atlantis is heavily guarded. I'm unsure if my father would appreciate me taking just anyone down there, especially the likes of Watts and Cook. I'm already bringing Marius and Jack. Papa sent me and my Sisters away two years ago, after we escaped from Nerissa, to keep the Sea Witch from moving on Atlantis. He'll do anything to protect his city.

Watts clicks his tongue a few times. The sound grates on my ears. "I can always stay here and wish you luck on fixing the vessel on your own. No big deal for me."

All eyes are on me. But losing my chance at Nerissa isn't really an option.

"What do you think, Sela?" Jack asks.

I glance at Cook; he's practically buzzing with energy. He knows that agreeing is the most advantageous decision at this point. Since, without Elijah, we can't fix the ship anytime soon. I take a deep breath and silently ask my father for forgiveness. "Fine. Watts, if you fix the *Scylla*, then you both can come."

Cook bobs his head with excitement a few times, and Watts lets out a satisfied chuckle.

"But Jack is going with you to the vessel," I say, adding to the deal.

Jack's eyes widen, and I narrow my eyes at him. I don't care if they dislike each other, Watts isn't going anywhere near my vessel or my home without supervision. And Jack is the strongest one here if there's an issue.

"Can I come?" Pearl pipes up.

"Of course." Jack takes her hand and waggles his eyebrows at me. "We'll have a party."

I try to smile at his sarcasm, but my lips freeze in a frown. Nerissa is going to Atlantis as a dig . . . a punishment for me. She probably sent Commander Thacher to kill Marius for the same reason.

Watts, Jack, and Pearl head for the front of the boat. I watch them for a second before turning away.

I press my finger up to the comm in my ear. "Una. Jack, Pearl, and the repair guy are boarding the Scylla to help."

"OK," she says, and the communication quickly cuts off. She's most likely working too.

"How about we check on my father?" Marius asks me.

I nod and walk alongside Marius, knowing he's trying to distract me. I welcome the diversion, at least for a little while.

Upon entering the room, I notice a difference in Thacher. He's still unconscious, but he doesn't look as menacing. I suppose that's mostly because he isn't trying to kill us. But it's also more than that. His natural color has started to return, and his scales aren't as thick, too, though still visible. He's resembling Marius's father more than the beast that we battled earlier. So, I guess, there's one positive right now. But we have a long way to go and apparently not enough hypospray to completely return him to normal.

Marius pulls up two chairs and places them near the bed. His eyes are on his father as he pats the seat next to him.

"It's going to be OK," I say, trying to muster up an ounce of positivity in this situation. But I have no idea if the statement is true. Or about anything, anymore.

"I know," he says. "I'm not worried about him. I'm worried about you."

I swivel in the chair, facing him. "Why are you worried about me? I'm not the one in a hospital bed."

Marius shrugs. "I mean, about going back to Atlantis. Pearl dropped that bomb on you and then we formed the plan. Not giving you much time to process."

"Do I need to process?"

"Do you?"

I sigh. Marius must totally see through me. "I don't know. I haven't seen my father in two years. I'm different now. And our reunion was . . . not what I had expected. I returned, hoping he would help. Instead, he ushered the girls and I out with the *Scylla*. I . . . I don't think he was even happy to see me."

"I'm sure he still loves you." Marius touches my arm. His fingers move downward until they intertwine with mine.

"I know. It's not just that."

"Then, what?"

I swallow the vessel-sized lump in my throat. "The last time I saw Nerissa? She said something that stuck with me."

Marius raises his eyebrows. "You're going to believe anything she has to say?"

"Not really. I know I shouldn't."

"I bet your father will be thrilled to see you this time."

"I don't think so," I admit. "After my mother died, Papa became busier at work, as if he was trying to avoid me for some reason. At least, that's how it felt. I wonder if coming home will remind him of my mother?"

Marius presses his lips together. I'm glad he doesn't tell me any different. I remember Papa pushing away from me, but I never blamed him.

"Do you have any good memories of Atlantis?" Marius asks.

"I guess. My freak-free childhood was good, actually. I did normal things, like go to school and explore the station." Recalling the memories of a revenge-free life tightens the muscles around my chest.

"Tell me," Marius leans in closer. "What's it like there?"

"Well, we had this deep-sea chamber that led away from the settlement. My mother and I used to go out together. We would find new and exciting flora and fish and then come back and research them. Memories of that helped after I became what I am now. I'm still reminded of her when I see something new or different under the surface."

"It sounds like you two were close."

He doesn't know much about my past, at least where my mother is concerned.

"We were." I smile, but it falters as I break from my memories and back to reality where she's dead, and Nerissa is about to invade my home. If she hasn't already.

"What happened to your mother?" Marius asks. "If you don't mind me asking?"

My heart beats nervously from the question. I haven't shared this with anyone. Ever. I tip my head and my hair falls over my shoulders. The color reminds me of hers. She always kept her hair long too. To this day, I remember her soft strands as I twirled strands around my fingers.

"I didn't understand much about her condition when I was a kid. Sometimes she would go from really happy and normal to locking herself in her room for hours or even a few days." My fingers tighten around Marius's, but he doesn't pull away. "Before Nerissa took me, I found my mother's journal. I knew it was wrong to read her private thoughts, but I wanted to feel closer to her again. Her words explained so much more than I ever thought possible."

"Like what?"

I draw in a shaky breath. "Her strange moods were caused by something called Deep Water Depression Syndrome. Living underwater in confinement on the settlement with artificial lighting affected her mind. She wrote about needing to return to the surface, but Papa fought with her to stay with us. He told her she would be fine with medication. But she wasn't."

I glance at the ceiling, blinking away the tears, but Marius doesn't stop me. "After Papa forced her to stay, the tone of her journal entries changed. They were more erratic. Even her handwriting turned messy and rushed as if she were writing in the dark or something. The sentences and words were sometimes jumbled too. She wrote about her nightmares and how she felt confined in her own body.

She wanted an escape. And she would do anything to get it."

"Did she go back to the surface?" Marius asks.

I shook my head, composing myself before uttering the words. "When it happened, no one would tell me much, other than she died. But from the journal, I knew her death must have been at her own hands. Which is why I think Papa buried himself in work. He blamed himself, I suppose. I don't know. We rarely spoke of her after that."

"Sela, I'm so sorry." Marius clutches my hand.

Staring at the edge of the bed, I nod. All the emotions from the day crash through me, but I don't stop the story there. "I'm sure it's why Papa sent me away two years ago. Or maybe he didn't want me to end up like her."

"But, it cost you your family."

"Yeah."

"I know I'm not a replacement—" He turns my head to face him. "But I won't ever force you away. I promise to be here for you."

"Thank you." A tear slips down my cheek. My shoulders drop as if an imaginary weight lifted from my body.

Marius presses his thumb against the tear and gently flicks it away. His hand opens, wrapping around the back of my neck as he pulls me closer.

He places a sweet gentle kiss on my lips, reminding me of how a few good things still exist. Electricity pulses through me as the world falls away. He starts to pull back, but I squeeze my eyes shut and reach out to him. A need for him to be closer overwhelms my body, and I fist the lapels of his jacket and bring him to me.

I melt into his kiss and, for that moment, I forget everything except the two of us.

CHAPTER 10

Sela

I'M THE FIRST to break the kiss. Marius opens his eyes, and a lazy smile remains on his lips. And just looking at him makes a flutter erupt in my chest. I squeeze his hand before I stand.

"You stay here. I'm going to check on the *Scylla's* progress."

He nods. "I'll be up soon."

"Don't rush. Be with your father. I'm sure he'll want to see you when he wakes up."

"Is this your way of not talking about us kissing?"

I smirk. "I don't have any regrets."

"Me either."

Resisting the urge to stay, I walk out of the room. But I want to give him a few minutes alone. If his father doesn't wake before we leave, then this might be the only chance he will have to speak to him before we leave for Atlantis.

On the main deck, I stride toward the bow, peering into the distance to find the *Scylla*. Without direct communication, I don't know the progress of the repairs. And, if I'm honest, there's a part of me that's in no hurry to get to Atlantis. I lean my arms against the railing, keeping my focus on the vessel bobbing up and down with the sea's movement.

Within a few minutes, a figure shoots up into the sky and heads back toward the *Echelon*. I stand straighter as Jack and Nyx fly toward me. Jack cradles Pearl in his arms, as effortlessly as he might carry Nyx. Jack touches down next to me and gently places Pearl on her feet.

"I'm not sure if I'll ever get used to that," Pearl says, beaming. Her thick hair is in a braid now, and she plays with the end.

Nyx zips around Jack's head and then lands on his shoulder.

"Any updates?" I ask.

Jack rakes a hand through his mussed hair. "The rest of the repairs are complete. Surprisingly, there wasn't much damage to the vessel's electronics."

"Good."

I hear the click of Cook's boots behind me before he joins our conversation. "Where's Watts?"

Jack hooks a thumb toward the *Scylla*. "He knows how to swim."

Cook lets out a grumble low in his throat.

"Seriously, Jack?" I smack him on the arm. "He's helping us repair the vessel. The least you can do is bring him back."

Jack shrugs. "He didn't want my help."

"You also didn't ask," Pearl adds.

"I thought you were on my side," Jack mutters.

"Go get him," I order.

Jack holds his hands up. "OK, OK!" He kisses Pearl on the cheek then lifts off from the ground. Nyx flies up to him before they take off for the vessel again.

"He thinks he's so funny," Cook says and then walks away from us.

Pearl smiles at me, and I try to match it but fail miserably. My stomach twists into an increasingly tighter knot as we get closer to setting sail for Atlantis.

"How are you doing with all of this?" Pearl asks as if she read my mind.

"I'm fine," I say quickly, and search my brain for a change of topic. "I bet it's nice to see Jack again." I roll my eyes. I should have come up with something better.

"Yes." She leans closer to me. "How about we take a walk around the deck? I'm a little nervous to be cooped up in that small vessel. I've had a lot of that the last few months."

I shrug and allow her to lead the way.

We don't walk too far before she starts talking. "I heard so many stories about Jack when I was held captive. Almost all of them made him out to be a bad person, but I never believed any of those tales. I always knew who he was."

"You love him."

She smiles to herself. "Love is a powerful thing."

I have no idea where she's going with all this. But talking is kind of the last thing I want to do.

Pearl places her hand on my arm and stops walking. "I don't know the full story with your dad, but I do know that love like what he and your mother shared will never die. That kind of bond is stronger than anything. Their story is legendary."

I clear my throat as a rising panic builds in my chest. I really don't want to be talking about *this*.

Pearl lifts her eyes to mine. "I was at a low point when I met Jack. I had just learned that my parents were lost at sea—probably dead. They went out scouting for land and just never came back. Jack stuck with me through all my pain. He helped me realize that the bond I shared with my parents will never fade. No matter what happens. It's unbreakable."

A breath catches in my throat as I think of Mama. "I'm sorry. I didn't know about your family."

She offers me a sad smile. "I'm just happy to be back with Jack."

"He's a different person around you. *Very* different from the boy I knew on Nerissa's research vessel."

"I must have tamed him," Pearl jokes in her bubbly voice.

I laugh, and my shoulders relax a notch. Then I open my mouth to tell her an incriminating tale about Jack when a loud *thud* interrupts the story.

Whipping around, I see a red-faced Watts pushing up from the deck. His teeth flash, and he glares up at Jack, who is hovering quite a distance in the air above him.

I sigh, and Pearl folds her arms, clearly not impressed with Jack's handling of Watts either.

"Come on," I say to Pearl, and we walk over to Watts.

The huge man is on his feet now, smacking his hands against his dirty pants. He's muttering incoherent words under his breath, probably cursing Jack out.

"Can we set sail?" I ask him.

"We're all set," he says. "Captain Cook and I need to gather some supplies, and then we'll be good to go."

"Thank you," I say to him, even though he weaseled a seat onto the vessel for his services.

Watts bobs his head and then takes off toward the bridge.

Once Watts is gone, Jack comes down to the deck. Pearl's eyes are drawn to him like a magnet.

"I'm going to check on Marius," I say.

Pearl nods and goes to Jack.

In the med bay, Thacher is in the same unconscious state while Marius still looks after him.

"Hi,"

"Hey," he says without turning around.

"The *Scylla* is all set. We're leaving shortly."

"I thought I'd be able to speak with him before we left," Marius says. "One of the medics came down and sedated him."

"What? Why?"

"For their protection." The corners of his mouth tug downward. "I understand. He did take out a fair amount of the crew. We have no idea what he'll be like when he wakes up."

"If you want to stay, I'll understand."

"No, I'm going. You can't get rid of me that easily."

A smile pulls at my lips. "You're sure?"

"Absolutely." He draws me against him. I close my eyes and take in the quiet moment before the storm.

***

Marius's hold steadies me as the small emergency boat cuts through the water toward the *Scylla*. Wind pulls back my hair.

Jack and Pearl fly above with Nyx at their side. Ethan pilots the boat as Marius, Cook, Watts, and I cram together on the tiny metal benches. Even though Cook and Marius get along, leaving Marius alone with Watts isn't the best idea. From the looks that Watts randomly shoots at Marius, he must be holding back resentment for when Marius was under the influence of Nerissa's serum.

Once we reach the *Scylla*, Cook and Watts are the first to disembark. The boat dips and then quickly rises as their excessive, combined weight leaves the craft. They head onto the vessel and then below deck. After I board, I turn back to the sea.

"Good luck," Ethan says, turning the boat around.

Jack hovers above the water, next to his friend.

"You're not coming?" I ask.

"He's going to be our eyes and ears on the *Echelon*," Jack says.

"And I've asked him to keep an eye on my father," Marius whispers.

Jack and Ethan bump fists before Ethan drives off toward the *Echelon* again. Ethan would do anything for his leader, but I wonder how he feels about being left behind.

Turning away from the water, the four of us and Nyx descend to the lower decks. On the bridge, I don't see Cook or Watts anywhere.

Una rushes over to me. "Everything good?"

"Yes," I say, removing the comm from my ear and handing it back to her.

"The comm came in handy, right?" she asks with a smug grin.

"You want me to say you were right?"

"It wouldn't hurt."

I roll my eyes. "Maybe another time. Where are Cook and Watts?"

Una's expression tightens. "In the kitchen."

"We should go check on them," Marius suggests.

"You OK here?" I ask Una.

Her eyebrows draw together. "Of course."

Inside the kitchen, Cook rummages around in the refrigerator while Watts searches the few cabinets. I'm about to tell them that we need to reserve our provisions when I notice that Cook is emptying food from a pack. Apparently, they brought their own supplies.

Marius and I cross the room toward the two tables and chairs taking up the rest of the space. Cook eyes us but says nothing. Maybe we interrupted something.

Watts brings several items of food to the small countertop and starts cutting a vegetable that I've never seen.

Cook walks over to us and takes a seat next to Marius. "I've met your father before, Sela."

I sit up straighter. "You have?"

Cook nods. His glasses fall farther down his nose, but he doesn't adjust them. He looks at me over the brim. "He came to my trading post once."

A million questions flood my mind. "Did you speak with him?"

Cook nods. "He was there for information on you and your Sisters."

"Why?" Marius asks.

My spine stiffens.

Cook leans back in his chair, crossing his arms. "He wanted to keep a close eye on you all without breaking Nerissa's treaty."

My mouth falls open. "What do *you* know about all that?"

"Not much," Cook answers. "What I do know is that none of Nerissa's deals are ever honest or simple. Evil stipulations are buried in every agreement, and always in her favor. When I was stationed at the Syndicate, Atlantis was off limits. As a successful underwater settlement, I found that odd. Nerissa never had any qualms about taking what she wanted, except when it came to Atlantis."

Was this why Papa sent me away so easily two years ago?

"We'll figure this all out when we get there," Marius says. "Right now, we need to focus on keeping Atlantis safe."

Or else I won't be able to get any answers.

My stomach growls as the savory aroma of whatever Watts is cooking wafts from the other side of the room. Craning my neck, I wonder if there is enough for us all. Even though Avalon has plenty of food, Cook always had the best meals.

When Watts comes over to the table, he places a plate in front of us with cooked fish meat sprinkled with seasoning and a green vegetable that looks like mini trees.

"Bon appetite," Watts says flatly.

While we eat, Cook and Watts talk about the boring operations of the *Echelon* in their absence, and my eyes start to close from the dull conversation and Marius's safe warmth.

Marius takes my hand and pulls me closer to him. I drop my head on his shoulder and give in to the sleep. I don't know if I'll get another chance. Cook and Watts's voices fade away as darkness claims me.

***

"We're here!" Pearl's voice cuts through the blackness of my mind. I jolt awake, jumping out of my chair. Marius grabs my arm to steady me.

Marius is the only other person in the room. Cook and Watts are gone. Pearl waves for us to follow and Marius and I look at each other for a brief moment.

"I won't leave you," he says.

"Not for a second?"

"Not for a second." He takes my hand and we race to the bridge where everyone stands by the sprawling, curved front window. Atlantis moves into view before us.

My stomach tenses as the illumination from Atlantis casts a blue hue over every surface inside of the *Scylla*. My gaze lifts, tracing the domed structures enclosing the towers and buildings of the settlement.

As we near, I step even closer to the windows. Outside of the settlement, the crumbling skyscrapers from before the water took over are still here. Those were the spots that Mama and I loved to explore outside of Atlantis.

I hold an image of her in my mind and don't let go as Una navigates the *Scylla* into a port.

CHAPTER 11

Sela

MY FINGERNAILS DIG into my palms. The tiny pricks of pain keep my hands from trembling as the side hatch of the *Scylla* opens in front of us. The pressurized *hiss* of the door fills my ears, revealing my childhood home inch-by-inch.

Una is by my side, but neither of us look at each other. We both know what coming back here means for me. I sense she wants to say something. But coming home must be overwhelming for her too.

As I requested, Cook and Watts are at the back of the group. I want to see Papa first and explain why I've brought all these people to our home. I'm almost positive their presence will be unwelcome. And then, when he and I are alone, I'm going to ask him all the hard questions.

Marius steps up beside me and his hand circles my wrist. He slides his hand into mine as the hatch reaches its highest point.

I inhale sharply.

A man stands on the other side. It takes me a second to recognize him since his beard has gone so gray. But his eyes are the same.

"Papa?" I breathe, stepping forward, but still maintaining my distance.

"Sela," he says and opens his arms to me. That's all I needed.

I rush into his embrace. Before he became distant, he always had a strong hug, and he doesn't disappoint this time. His hand presses my head to his chest. His strong heart beats against my cheek.

After a few moments, he releases me and then steps toward the others. I stick to his side, ready to explain who I've brought to our home and why.

"Una," Papa says, and then he embraces her too. Una releases a breath as Papa pushes his shoulders back and stands in front of her as if he's protecting her from our companions.

His gaze touches everyone, and it narrows slightly when he gets to Cook and Watts. He turns to me, keeping his eyes on the others. "As much as I'm happy to see you two return home, I'm a little confused. It isn't safe for you to be here. If discovered, Nerissa will come to Atlantis."

"She's already on the way," I say.

Papa's thick eyebrows knit together. "What are you talking about?"

I toss a glance at Pearl. "Nerissa is coming for Atlantis. Pearl heard their plan before we won back Avalon."

Papa looks at her, narrowing his brow. He strokes his beard a few times. "This is most concerning. We haven't heard anything about her movements in some time. I suppose I should have seen this coming."

"We came to warn you," Una says.

Papa nods. "Well, you're here now, so I might as well let you in to discuss the matter further." He turns on his heels, and I'm right by his side, almost forgetting about all my apprehension to come to Atlantis. Almost.

"Nyx, stay here and secure the *Scylla*," Jack says from behind.

Glancing over my shoulder, I see Nyx flutter around and then stop to hover in front of Jack with her little arms crossed over her chest. Her optics narrow into slits.

"Go," Jack orders.

She lets out a short huffing sound and then flies back on board our vessel.

I wipe my clammy hands against my thighs. The last time we were at this port, my Sisters and I were fleeing for our lives. Coming back brings a heavy weight to my chest as we travel through the sprawling hyperloop system that connects everything within Atlantis.

I glance out of the glass windows and viewing ports as we glide through the transport tubing. Flickers of memories with Mama overwhelm me and heat pricks at the back of my eyes.

The docking port corridor is narrow but quickly opens to fifteen-foot-tall ceilings. There have been several upgrades in my absence. Papa must have dug himself even deeper into his work. We exit the hyperloop pod and continue on foot now.

My father seems lost in his thoughts, so I give him a chance to sort through them. Instead, I inspect the changes in the life-sustaining domed habitats in the distance. I smile as I check out the entrance to the LED vertical farming habitat. My Sisters and I would get into trouble as children when we hid among the countless rows of crops, playing hide-and-seek.

I glance at Una; a smile forms on her lips as if she's reading my mind.

As we continue walking, no one speaks. We all look around at my home with curious expressions. Especially since this place is heavily guarded to keep strangers away.

Pearl grips Jack's hand and I try not to notice the secretive glances between Cook and Watts. I have no idea what they have planned, but I doubt Papa will let them wander off on their own to do whatever shady business they have in mind.

The corridor narrows again as we reach the command center. Papa presses his hand against the digital display outside of the door. His handprint illuminates before a loud *click* sounds, and the door swings open. The operations deck is dim and blinking lights wink at us throughout the space. Once we're all inside, the door closes, and one of the officers stands at attention next to it.

I barely get a glimpse of his face when someone calls out to me.

"Sela!"

I whip around and meet two big, sparkling brown eyes. At the sight, I'm tossed back in time.

"Celia?"

She smiles and then wraps her arms around my shoulders. "It's so good to see you again."

"You too," I say, unable to stop smiling.

"I heard you were docking. But, wow, I can't believe it." She's dressed in an officer's uniform, and her blonde hair is tied back into a tight bun. I remember she always fought her mom over not wanting to wear her hair up as a kid. She glances around at our group and must notice Papa's stern expression.

"Sir," she says and bows her head.

"You're in the command center now?" I lean in to ask her. It's obvious by how she's dressed, but I can't help but want to know more.

"Yes," she says stiffly. "Anyway, we'll catch up later, OK?"

"Of course," I say, and then she backs away from us, her eyes never leaving Papa.

He has that effect on a lot of people. Not me, though.

Papa leads us into the closed war room in the middle of the command center. I've never been inside before. As far as I knew, only Papa and higher officers were allowed.

I swallow hard and walk inside. Besides a few thin pieces of glass breaking up the walls, there are no other views of anything outside the room. Beams of light reach up from the perimeter of the floor, illuminating the room and the large circular table in the center. There are easily a dozen chairs surrounding the table.

"Take a seat," Papa instructs and then takes the larger chair at the back of the room.

I sit next to him, and Una plops down in the chair next to me. Cook and Watts are the farthest away, probably for the best.

"Now, I want to discuss the last thing anyone knows about Nerissa's whereabouts," Papa says. "At least then, we can have a starting place."

"The last time we saw her was on Avalon," I say, starting the conversation.

Jack and Marius nod almost in unison. Watts and Cook remain silent and Papa hasn't even acknowledged them yet. Maybe he doesn't remember Cook from the trading post.

My father draws in a breath and leans back in his chair. "I've heard reports that she has several vessels docked in undisclosed locations. She's most likely rearmed her forces by now."

"She's planning on taking over Atlantis," Jack says, glancing at Pearl. "We think she's planning to make it her new base of operations. Now that she doesn't have control over Avalon."

Papa shakes his head, and his hands curl into fists.

"She won't find Avalon for quite some time. . . if ever," Jack says. "The settlement was moved."

"Atlantis is the only logical target," I say.

"Is she able to get here?" Marius asks. "Without Avalon's resources—"

"I gave her a few submersibles," Papa interrupts.

Cook clears his throat, and Papa shoots him a look. "It was part of the treaty."

The treaty that sent me and my Sisters away when we came back for help two years ago. My mouth dries up, and I lick my lips, trying to appear unfazed. I'm sure it's not working.

Papa smooths down his beard again and stands up. He reaches over to a small electrical box attached to the table and presses a button. Seconds later, the door opens, and we all turn to see an officer standing at the ready.

"Contact our connections on the nearby settlement cruise liners to see if they have any new intel," Papa orders.

"Yes, sir," the officer says.

"Also," Papa says. "Deploy our fleet to surround Atlantis and be on alert for my orders."

"Very well, sir," the officer says and then turns on his heels and leaves the room.

"We can take the *Scylla* out too," Marius says. "It will give you and Sela a chance to reconnect."

Marius gives me a weighted look. He knows I want to speak with Papa and this is the best opportunity. Once we find Nerissa, we're going to have bigger problems.

"You don't need us, right," Watts asks.

Jack snorts. "You're kidding, *right?*"

Watts scoffs.

"Whoever wishes to remain in the settlement can," Papa says.

Cook and Watts share a look of interest.

I open my mouth to tell Papa that might not be wise.

"But if you do," Papa says before I get out any words. "You will stick to the public zones and will be escorted by my officers."

The smug looks on Cook and Watts faces fall.

"If there's nothing else?" Papa asks, dismissing everyone.

Marius doesn't dare kiss me in front of Papa, but he does lightly squeeze my arm before leaving the room with Una, Jack, and Pearl in tow.

Cook and Watts stand by and wait for Papa to assign two guards. The four officers on either side of Cook and Watts don't look pleased at all, but Papa's men don't dare speak back to him. The chosen two escort them.

Once everyone is out of the room, Papa turns to me. A smile peeks out from under his beard, but the expression doesn't quite reach his eyes.

"I want to speak with you," I say, not wanting to delay any further.

"I had a feeling you might." He places a hand on my shoulder. "Let's find somewhere else private to talk."

Papa doesn't need to lead me anywhere. The only private place we have together is my former home. Instead of living with the rest of the residents in the living habitat, Papa had chosen for us to live near the command center. The Executive Quarters are much bigger than the rest of the habitats, but it's isolated. It's one reason I was rarely there when I lived in the settlement. I always preferred to be with others while Papa surrounded himself with work.

I follow him, and we make our way down a long corridor off from the command center. The familiar metal door at the end of the hall floods me with euphoria. Upon entering the space, I inhale sharply. A sweet scent fills my nose, and I instantly turn to see the fresh flowers on the console table in the hall. It's as if I never left. We don't grow many species since the farming space is mostly used for life-sustaining foods, but flowers are used for special events in Atlantis. Papa gave them to Mama on occasion too. She would save the flowers by placing them between the pages of a notebook. The scent would cling to our home for weeks. He's kept this tradition alive.

"Are you coming?" Papa asks.

I blink and pull myself out of the memory. Walking into the small entryway, I glance around. Papa hasn't changed much. Though, the small tabletop near the door is empty.

Mama used to place little mementos there. Where could they be?

It appears as if only essentials fill his space now. Did those things remind Papa of what he had done? Swirls of guilt move through me, but I don't lose my nerve.

Stopping at the end of the hallway, I stare out through the front windows overlooking Atlantis.

Papa is in the kitchen. He pours two glasses of water before handing one to me. He leans back against the counter and stares into his glass.

I can almost see the faint outline of Mama moving around the kitchen in front of him. She used to dance around the room as she cooked, encouraging me to do the same. We would sing and dance until even Papa joined us sometimes, although that always took more than a little coaxing.

I smile. Being away from here and thinking of her always brought up the sad memories. But inside of our home, I can only think of the good times. I wish I could bottle that feeling and take it with me.

"I've missed you, Sela," Papa says. His voice is low and soft. "I never meant for all of this to happen."

I blink, and the ghost in my mind disappears from the room. It's only him and me now. "I want to know about the treaty."

Papa opens his mouth to speak, but I jump in first. "The truth."

"I know, little minnow," Papa says. "I won't spare you any longer."

I cross my arms over my chest and wait for whatever he has to say. I'm not a minnow anymore.

"I did something stupid. A long time ago." He swipes a hand over his face and then takes another sip of water. "I was swayed by Nerissa when you were just a baby."

"What?" I ask, leaning forward.

Papa puts a hand in the air, and I bite down on my lip to keep from speaking over him.

"Nerissa made her work seem as if it were going to save humanity. You need to realize that at the time, the world was in chaos. She offered hope."

"Papa, what did you do?" My chest tenses at the possibilities.

"I created a protocol that mandated a lottery system for the people of Atlantis. It forced families with multiple children to enter the lottery and allow Nerissa to experiment on their children."

A breath catches in my throat, and my entire body is frozen.

"I didn't know the extent of what Nerissa was doing. Eventually, I noticed the children weren't returning to their homes."

"Papa," my voice comes out breathy.

He tightens his jaw. "It nearly destroyed our settlement. There were revolts. The citizens of Atlantis nearly took down my position and the settlement."

"What did you do?"

"As much as Nerissa had caused all of these issues, she was the only one who had enough manpower and resources to regain order."

"So, why did you keep going with her program?"

"It was the only choice she gave me. I couldn't stop her from doing what she had already done, but she threatened Atlantis as a whole. I wanted to protect you, Sela. And your mother. I had to keep Atlantis alive. This place is one of a kind. Allowing our settlement to fall wasn't a possibility."

"Are you saying that you allowed Nerissa to take me as one of her test subjects?"

"No," Papa says, stepping forward. He reaches out for my hand, but I pull away from him. His shoulders sag. "You weren't supposed to be taken. It was an accident. The one thing I regret the most. By the time I realized what had happened, you were already gone."

"You left me with her?" Tears fill my eyes. Why didn't he fight for me?

"I tried to get you back, but Nerissa saw potential in you and refused."

I sniff and press my hands to my cheeks, wiping away my tears, unable to believe what I'm hearing.

"She threatened us, Sela. She threatened Atlantis. What was I supposed to do? If I pursued you, then Nerissa would have destroyed this place. There wouldn't have been a home for us to return to. Worst of all, she placed a lockdown on the settlement that stayed for years."

He knew where I was and couldn't come for me.

"The plan had been in place to take back my settlement," Papa says. "When you broke free, it was the very sign we needed to rise up. I took back Atlantis and ended the child-experiment program once and for all. We fought with the Syndicate for months before making a new treaty."

"Then why did you let me go after I escaped?"

Papa's gaze dips to the floor. "You were a part of the treaty."

"Because Nerissa saw *potential* in me?"

Papa nods slowly as if the very movement pains him. "If you ever returned to Atlantis, the Syndicate would return to finish us. After all the experiments, Nerissa claimed you for the Syndicate."

"So . . . you sent me away."

Papa's breaths come quickly. He drops his glass of water onto the counter, and the liquid sloshes over the rim. "Sela—I'm—" his hands reach up to his face, and he chokes on his breath. "I'm so sorry." His legs give out from under him, and his knees crash to the floor with a sickening *crack.*

I stare at my Papa, never seeing him so overcome by emotion before. My chest heaves as his sobs fill the room.

CHAPTER 12

Sela

"Papa, please," I say, coming to his side.

He's still on the floor, and he throws his hand out for me to stop.

I halt mid-stride and watch him to unsuccessfully hide his emotion from me. He wipes at his tear-soaked cheeks and my own eyes begin to water.

Not once have I ever seen him like this. Not even after Mama died.

Tears soak the long whiskers of his gray beard. "I'm fine, little minnow."

He stands, straightening his shoulders. Tiny red veins outline the whites of his eyes, but his impassive expression returns. It's the one that I remember leaving behind all those years ago.

Our cabin shrinks around me and my heart hammers in my ears—the urge to run back to my friends claws at me.

"I should go," I say. "And, um, check on the others." It's just an excuse to go, but he won't question.

Papa nods, but the corners of his eyes soften. "I'll see you soon."

Outside of the cabin door, I'm alone and able to take a full breath. Seeing Papa crack under the pressure of the truth is as overwhelming as the truth itself. He had signed a treaty with Nerissa to take people's children. Their children! No wonder there was a revolt. Nerissa had a lot of power behind her, but there must have been another way that wouldn't have involved innocent lives.

Tears prick at my eyes, thinking of other, younger kids going through what Jack and I had at some other remote testing location.

Jack. The others. How can I tell them what Papa had done? Una will never look at him the same. Is there a way to keep all of this to myself?

Without a destination in mind, I walk for a little while. But my legs lead me to the one place I need right now.

I run my hand over the curved glass of the viewing port, once the perfect size for a smaller me. The glass is smooth under my fingers and slightly cool to the touch. It's the one place I went when I wanted to be alone with my thoughts. So, it's no surprise that I ended up here now.

Brightly colored marine life swim by the port's dim outer lights, and my shoulders relax. I used to count the number of fish passing by. Sometimes, when I was particularly upset, I would make sure to count a hundred fish before returning to our pod. Two hundred would probably be appropriate today.

But before I find thirty fish, boot steps clomp from behind me. I'm not ready to speak with Papa again so soon.

I turn, but it's not Papa.

"Sela," Celia says. "I didn't think anyone would be out here."

I shove my hair over my shoulders, attempting to plaster on a smile. "Oh, I was just checking out a few of the places I remember. It's nice to be home."

She returns my smile. "I didn't think I would see you again."

I sigh. "Me either."

Celia glances at her shiny black shoes then up at me. I don't think I'm doing a good job of hiding my feelings.

"I'm on my break. Did you want to get something to eat? I'm heading over to the commerce sector."

"Sure." At the very least, it's a distraction for me until Marius and the others return. The blueprint of Atlantis is so ingrained in my mind that I don't have to think about where to walk.

"So, how did you get to work in the command center?" I ask

"It was the highest-ranking career after taking final exams," she says. "My parents were so proud. I couldn't tell them that I wanted to be a—"

"Professor," we say in unison.

She smirks. "You remember."

I bump her shoulder. "Of course, I do. When we played, you were always the teacher."

"Testing into the command center is a great honor. I'm lucky to have been chosen."

The air between us shifts and I know she must want to ask me about what I've been up to. No doubt there's been rumors circulating. But I'm not sure if I'm ready to give my side just yet.

Before she gets the chance, I ask her about the changes in Atlantis. As a member of the command center, she knows more than most when it comes to developments, ones not disclosed to civilians. Turns out, there's been a lot of changes in my absence. Papa has been actively shifting policy to include civilians in shaping the future of Atlantis. Giving them voting rights and a seat at the table in a sense. He's been trying hard to regain their trust, but Celia says it's been tough. The people have been slow to accept him as their leader again.

My mood sours. I don't want to talk about my father or what happened in the past. Luckily, Celia is on the same page as me.

"You're not going to believe the developments of the commerce sector," Celia says, breaking me from my thoughts. "It's so much cleaner and easier to navigate than when we were kids."

"Really?" That was the fun of the commerce section. We would ditch our parents within seconds of arriving and then play silly games together while the adults did all the tedious shopping.

Once we reach the commerce sector, it's as if I'm walking into an entirely new place. Metal barriers used to separate the stalls, but now each section has a storefront with signs hanging over the top of each stall. Celia was right about the cleanliness. The floors aren't sticky and now made of slick tiles that feel a little springy under my feet. I'm glad she offered to take me here.

Citizens of Atlantis mill around, stopping at their favorite clothing and food stalls—at least a dozen in total. Almost double what I remember.

No one stops to gape at me, which is a good thing. I don't want to alert anyone to possible danger before the real threat arrives. I'm sure most people know that I'm one of the missing kids, so any notice of my return will immediately connect them with worries over Nerissa.

The thought sends a shiver down my spine.

"I know coming back must be confusing for you." Celia apparently notices my shift in demeanor and leads me to a bench. "During Nerissa's Syndicate years, Atlantis wasn't like this at all. People didn't smile or live free lives. Most of the time, we were on lockdown with little hope of knowing a life like we do now. It's part of the reason I took this job." She tucks her hands into the pockets of her uniform pants. "There wasn't an option. All of us had to come together to save this place from Nerissa. And Commander Tritus has dedicated himself to bringing you back home, and to end this conflict for good."

"He has?" I ask and sit.

Celia joins me and pats my shoulder. "He loves you." She glances around then her eyes lift to mine. "This is probably breaking protocol, but I'm going to tell you anyway." She scoots closer and lowers her voice. "He's spent countless off-hours working on solutions to this. He's suffered so much. I'm not going to tell you what to do since I know that doesn't work against your stubbornness, but maybe you should give him a break. Or at least think about it from his point of view."

I exhale slowly and my shoulders relax. "You're right." Needing to get out of this state of mind, I stand up and pull Celia with me. "I'm not going to take up any more of your break. You must be hungry."

Celia grins. "And I know just the place."

We meld into the crowd and I peer into one of the stalls, recognizing the clothing right away.

"Mareesh is still selling these scarves, huh?" I ask Celia.

"Her daughter runs the shop now. Mareesh died last year."

I touch one of the colorful scarves at the edge of the store. "She was a sweet lady."

I take a few steps, still looking back at the stall, but almost crash into Celia when she abruptly stops in front of me. "Whoa, sorry—?"

Looking at the sign above us, my nose is flooded with another scent that sends me way back to my childhood.

"I don't believe this is still here," I say, pressing my hands against the glass partition. On the other side, a young guy—wearing a white apron and a hairnet over his thick, black hair—prepares prawn and scallop skewers for the grill. Memories of the most amazing sauces drizzled over each little bite of heaven tingle on my tongue.

"We're getting one," I say, shoving over to the order counter.

"We're getting two," Celia says. "I'm not sharing."

I laugh and face a frowning older man who sits in front of me.

"Whaddaya want?" he grunts.

I blink. "Mr. Boyd?"

He peers over his glasses. "Yeah?" He was even old and grumpy when I was a kid.

"Two number fours, please," Celia says since my mouth seems to be watering too much to form words.

Mr. Boyd presses his wrinkly fingers against the small electronic pad in front of him and gives the price for the order. I touch my pockets and remember that I don't have any money. Atlantis credits are useless on the open sea.

Celia reaches forward and swipes a white card over the surface. "You get me next time."

I press my lips together. Hopefully, there's a next time.

Mr. Boyd leans over to the guy who's now stirring some sort of green sauce. "Two number four sticks!" he shouts about five times louder than necessary.

The young guy rolls his eyes. I'm not sure if Mr. Boyd is deaf or just likes to yell. Either way, his employee isn't impressed.

"Some things never change, huh?" I mutter.

I catch Celia's eye and we both break into a giggle. Mr. Boyd scowls.

I rub my hands together as I anticipate that first morsel. Just as Mr. Boyd is about to hand us our order, an alarm rips through the habitat. All the patrons stop in their tracks and then take off in different directions.

"I have to go," Celia says, her eyes wide and fearful.

"I'm coming with you."

Leaving our snack behind, we sprint off toward the command center. I slow my pace a little for her to keep up with me. My heart pounds in my chest with each step.

Has Nerissa already found us?

Once we reach the command center, Celia places her hand on the electronic pad to the side of the door. The door swings open and we rush inside. Papa is at the helm where there are more blinking lights than there were before, and most are an intense red.

Without a goodbye, Celia takes her spot at her station.

"What's going on?" I ask as I dash over to Papa's side.

He twists around to face me. "We've spotted Nerissa's vessels."

CHAPTER 13

Jack

OFF IN THE distance, through the *Scylla*'s curved front window, the outline of Atlantis's submersible vessel is the only thing visible in this murky water. I'm not a passenger on the targeted ship, but my palms are sticky with sweat all the same.

I jump as a bright light illuminates the water, and then the ship's outline is gone. The vessel that was just intact is now probably in a million pieces. I cringe and rub my hands over the armrest of the chair.

I glance at Una. Her eyes narrow in as she concentrates on the radar screen in front of her, since the visibility is next to nothing this deep.

Marius stands next to her with arms crossed. He stares at the radar, as silent and still as a statue.

The circle indicating the targeted vessel blinks out from the display, and Una taps on the controls to locate the target.

Hopefully, it's not us.

Another deep pop echoes from outside of the hull.

Una pulls her head up. "Another Atlantis vessel is gone." She curses under her breath. "We don't have enough firepower to fight them all off, but we can't go back and leave Atlantis unguarded."

Nyx flits around my head. Her eyes blink through all the colors in her interface.

"I know we're in danger," I say and shoo her away. Nyx is causing my pulse to spike, and I don't need her anxiety on top of everything else.

With a pout, she settles on one of the higher shelves across the room. Her body is still, but her eyes continue to flicker.

I glance at Pearl. Her hand clutches the top of my chair and her eyes narrow and widen as if she's trying to see through the dark water. I'm sure her efforts are futile. I'm enhanced and can't see crap out there.

The *Scylla* jerks to the left, and I reach out for Pearl before she falls on top of me.

Una is knocked back in her chair and quickly grabs onto the operations station to regain her balance. Marius holds her chair in place, steadying himself.

"You alright?" he asks Una.

Una doesn't look up. "If you were able to read this radar, you would know that there wasn't any warning. Not with their technology. The strikes are almost invisible until they're right on top of us."

A wave of debris presses against the front window. Another blast from the Syndicate, which also means another Atlantis vessel is down.

"No, no, no," Una says as two blinking lights on the screen go dark.

The *Scylla* rocks backward from the blast, and I wrap my arm around Pearl's waist as the vessel moves upward this time.

"Hold on." Una moves several of the controls simultaneously until we're level again.

I stand up from my chair and move to get a better look at the sensors.

Pearl turns to Una. "Is there anything we can do?"

Most of my abilities are useless underwater, and I can't help but regret bringing Pearl along with us. Visions flash before my eyes, of Nerissa's forces blowing the *Scylla* into smithereens, of the end of everything.

"What's that light?" Marius points to the radar screen.

Una leans in closer.

"Why's it blue?" Marius asks.

"It's an Atlantis vessel. The electronics are disabled. But the ship is still functional," Una says.

"What does that mean?" Pearl asks.

Marius looks over at us with a small smile. "It means we can help."

"Help them?" I ask. "That's a suicide mission?"

Una whirls around at me. "This isn't *the* battle. This is only Nerissa breaching the Atlantis forces. We need to preserve as many of their crafts as we can. So yes, we're going to help. If you don't like it, I'll open the side hatch. Feel free to swim out of here."

"What if we come in from behind?" Marius suggests. "The Syndicate will only see one indicator, and we can make a surprise move."

"It's a good plan," Una says, although her voice suggests she's not completely convinced. "Hold on, people."

The murky water moves across the front window as Una blindly directs our vessel toward the damaged Atlantis ship.

Pearl holds onto me a little tighter, and I squeeze back.

Any other time, I would have been ready for this fight. Ready to defend my friend and her home. Now, all I want is Pearl safe. Always.

Rubbing my hand across my face, I shake away the thoughts. We offered to come out here and fight against Nerissa. That's the plan.

I stand and grab Pearl to pull her alongside me. Then we step closer to Una's station, who is busy pressing a few buttons. All the lights in the cabin turn off, except for the now dull glow of her station.

"We can't give off any signal until the right moment," she says.

Marius leans closer to Una. "They're circling."

"What's happening?" Pearl's voice is harsh against my ear. She's a brave girl, but both of us are helpless, relying on Una and Marius to take down the targeted Syndicate vessel.

"We're waiting until they make their move," Marius says. "They're as blind as we are."

"But they've managed to take down a slew of Atlantis vessels so far," I say.

"Thanks for stating the obvious," Una says without turning around.

"You're welcome," I say.

Pearl jabs me in the side, and I peck her on the cheek. My hand tightens around her shoulder as my gaze narrows on the radar screen.

"There's one," Marius says.

"Got it." On the screen, Una taps her finger on a yellow circle surrounding a red dot.

"Keep steady," Marius whispers.

"I've got this, relax," Una snaps.

Marius presses his lips together and backs off a few inches.

"Is there any way we can help the other vessel?" Pearl asks.

"Not yet," Una says. "We need to neutralize the threat before we can be of any assistance."

The blinking light on the screen comes closer to our location. Una's hand hovers over the trigger switch. I'm assuming she's going to blast them when the ship is close enough.

But when the red dot hits the inner ring of the coordinates, the dot disappears.

Una gasps. "What the—?"

"Where did they go? They take a hit?" Marius asks.

"No," Una says. "There's no one in their vicinity. Unless—"

Her words cut off as the entire vessel shakes violently. I grab for Pearl as we crash to the floor.

Marius skids across the room on the floor, while Una lets out a guttural sound as she holds onto her operation station. Somehow Nyx buzzes in the air, maintaining a perfect hover.

"What's happening?" I shout as a deafening booming fills the room.

"They're targeting us from behind," Una calls. She taps frantically, but the vessel is out of her control.

I plant my legs firm into a side panel to keep me and Pearl from whipping across the room.

Marius peels himself off the ground and crawls toward Una.

The *Scylla* is shifting so fast, I have no idea of our direction. The motion is disorienting.

"Where are they?" Marius asks when he reaches his seat.

"I don't know!" Una says. "Their ship is moving too quickly. Like it has cloaking technology."

I glance out the window. Billows of sand, and whatever else from the ocean floor, cloud our vision. We need to hide. Just like the attacking vessel. But how? Nerissa and her damn upgrades.

"Can you stop this thing?" I ask.

"Stop?" Una asks, whipping her head in my direction. "You think I'm making this happen?"

I click my tongue, not willing to argue with her. "If the radar isn't working, then we need to do something else. We need to let the dust settle so we have eyes on the enemy."

Una glances at Marius.

He shrugs. "Not a bad idea. Can we do it?"

Una chews on her lip hard enough that I think she's going to draw blood.

A blast hits the side of the *Scylla* again, and the entire cabin shudders.

Pearl screeches and holds onto me tighter.

"What are we doing, guys?" I ask.

"They already know we're here," Una says. "If we disable all systems, they might think we're down for good."

"Won't they make sure of that?" Marius asks.

Una steels herself. "There's only one way to find out."

She maneuvers the *Scylla* until we touch down on the ocean floor. Then she presses almost every single button on her operations panel, shutting everything off to mask our signal. She glances out the window, and my eyes glue to the same place.

My heart pounds as if it's going to beat right out of my chest.

"I think it's working," Una says.

In the distance, an outline of a vessel appears.

"Can you turn on the weapons without the ship noticing?" Marius asks.

"We can try," Una says. "But the ship's location on our radar is inconsistent."

I grit my teeth and think of every curse word in the world, mentally throwing them at the Sea Witch.

The Syndicate vessel inches toward us as if knowing our plan.

My breathing intensifies as my core tightens. I wish I could be in the air to personally tear the enemy apart.

"Here goes nothing," Una says and then flips open the clear plastic cover on the trigger.

She's about to press down when the Syndicate vessel explodes in a cloud of brilliant orange.

Instinctively, I throw my hand to my eyes to block the blinding light.

I blink away the phantom image after the orange flickers out. The outline of the vessel disappears as shrapnel disappears into the upwelled, murky water.

"Did you fire?" Marius asks Una.

"No," she says. "Wasn't me."

I rush to the front window and peer out into the vast ocean, but I still can't see a thing in the sea haze.

"All communications are coming back online on the Atlantis vessel," Una says.

Pressing my hands against the glass, I'm able to finally take a measured breath. That is until something resembling a human face appears in the window. I stumble back.

Sela.

I release a shaky breath, thankful she wasn't a decapitated head of a Syndicate member.

Her red hair flows around her like a fiery crown. Then she sticks her tongue out at me and waves.

I have the urge to make an inappropriate gesture at her as payback for scaring the crap out of me, but, I'm too relieved to be angry.

She swims over ahead of Una and points to the back of the *Scylla*.

Una clicks a few buttons, and Sela swims out of sight.

"Marius," Una says, "let her in the hatch."

Marius sprints out of the cabin.

A couple of minutes later, Sela and Marius come onto the bridge. Sela is soaking wet and doing her best to dry off with a towel.

"It's about time you got here," I say

Sela shoots me a smirk. "Thought you could use a little help."

"We were handling it," Una says, staring at her radar. She grabs the comm from the side of the panel. When she clicks it on, a voice fills the room.

"Atlantis, anyone, do you read me?" A female voice crackles through the comm. "This is the *Atlantis Raptor*. We're targeted by the Syndicate and need immediate assistance."

CHAPTER 14

Sela

"Do you copy?" the female voice continues. "This is the *Atlantis Raptor*; we need assistance. Over."

Shoving my soaking wet hair over my shoulder, I stride over to Una's station, grabbing the comm. I raise my thumb to press the button when someone touches my arm.

"Wait," Jack says.

I whip around to face him. "What is it?"

"We should think about this. We were almost blown up a minute ago for helping someone."

"Isn't that why we're here?"

"Well, yeah, but—"

"If you don't want to be here, leave," I say through my teeth.

"Already told him that," Una says without looking up from her station.

Jack glances at Pearl and then lifts his chin. "I'm not leaving. Let's take a second to think about this."

"There isn't time to think," I say, pressing my finger on the button on the side of the comm. *This is my home. And I'll protect Atlantis at all costs.*

"This is the *Scylla*," I say into the comm. "*Raptor*, what are your coordinates?"

I release the button and wait.

Marius squeezes my arm, but I don't reach back. The wreckage outside of the *Scylla* would cause any sane person to run. Instead, we hold our positions.

The voice rings over the speakers again, spouting off the coordinates of their vessel. The woman repeats the coordinates two more times, but I know Una had them on the first try. She goes to work, homing on the vessel on her screen.

Outside the window, the debris has settled quite a bit, but we won't be able to get to them without a radar. At least not as quick as they need.

"Three Syndicate boats surround us," the voice says. "We're pinned against the North side of Atlantis. If we move, our comm towers will be compromised."

Una lifts her gaze to mine. "How do you want to do this?"

I chew on my bottom lip and glance at Marius. His shoulders are back, ready to do whatever I'm about to ask of him.

Hesitation flits through Jack's eyes, but I don't have time to worry about him. My home is in danger, and *all* my friends signed up to help the moment they stepped onto the *Scylla*.

"Swing around and we'll come in from the South side," I order to Una. "If their focus is on the *Raptor*, they'll have to choose to protect themselves or the mission."

Una nods.

"We're on our way," I say into the comm, and then place it down.

Immediately, Una lurches the vessel forward. We race through the bluish-gray ocean. Large chunks of shrapnel sit on the ocean floor, remnants of the terrible devastation from both sides of this fight.

My stomach churns and my hands ball into fists. Turning away, I focus on the radar screen, studying our progress toward the *Raptor*.

Our indicator light darts across the screen as the light for the *Raptor* blinks. The red Syndicate vessels are too close to the Atlantis vessel. We need to get there in time.

No one speaks. The only sounds filling the cabin are the various beeps coming from the operation station. I almost want to push Una out of her seat, so I can steer. But I know that if push comes to shove, I'm more effective outside of the *Scylla*.

"There they are," Jack says, sprinting toward the window.

The murkiness clears as the lights from Atlantis illuminate the four vessels ahead.

My breath hitches.

The *Raptor* floats in front of one of the leading operational towers. If the Syndicate seizes control, we might as well give up.

No, not going to happen.

The *Raptor* bobs up and down as the Syndicate vessels attempt to move closer as if they're playing a game of cat and mouse.

"Be careful not to fire near the *Raptor*," I say to Una.

"No kidding."

I grit my teeth. I don't have time for her attitude.

"What if we lead one of their vessels away?" Marius suggests.

"How do we know they won't just blow up the *Raptor* at that point?" Jack asks.

I force out a breath. "We don't. Una, fire at the farthest one. Just in case we miss."

"It's nice to know that you have faith in my abilities," she says.

"I have faith, but I want to be cautious," I say.

"Aye, aye," she says and then moves the *Scylla* into position.

We're close enough that the Syndicate vessels must know we're in range, but none move out of position. This plan has to work, or we could be diving into a trap.

My entire body vibrates as all my nerves fire. I wrestle to keep as calm as possible. Una needs to concentrate.

She fires, and I feel the rippling tremor under my feet. The targeted Syndicate vessel shoots upward, faster than I've ever seen one move. Our torpedo shoots off into the vast ocean, completely missing our target.

Nyx chirps frantically, trying to hold onto the shelf.

I turn to see a wide-eyed Pearl. "Jack, take her to the back."

But before I even notice if he obeys, another torpedo fires from below and the *Scylla* bucks. I grab onto Una's station and my gaze darts between the radar screen and the front window.

Both Syndicate vessels disappear to either side of us.

"Hold on!" Una says and turns the vessel.

I almost wish the water was as clouded as it had been when I boarded the vessel.

Movement from the vessels' hull catches my eye. The Syndicate cannons move into position, pointing right at us.

The *Scylla* drops, along with my stomach. The Syndicate vessels disappear as Una steers us underneath. She targets the closest one and fires off two shots.

Neither hit.

In the span of a heartbeat, the Syndicate vessels are on us again. This time, they don't hesitate. Both ships fire at the same time.

Una shifts the *Scylla* to the side, but the entire vessel rumbles. Several sensors blink red and don't stop. She lets out a growl and moves us away from the enemy.

"We're in their sights," I say, watching the radar. And close enough that, with one or two more hits, we'll go down.

"Lead them away," Jack says. "Maybe the *Raptor* can handle itself against one. We have the speed."

I wheel around toward him. "I thought I told you to go in the back?"

Jack doesn't budge as Pearl still stands at his side, wide-eyed. I shake my head.

"They're going to know what we're doing," I say. "They want the comm tower and will go back unless—"

"Unless what?" Marius asks.

I move away from the station and turn to face them as the plan forms in my mind. "I'm going out there."

"No, you're not," Jack and Marius say at the same time.

The boys look at each other in shock over agreeing to the same thing.

"I can maneuver faster than the Syndicate ships can," I say. "I'll get their attention. I'll be a distraction."

"Yeah, but you forgot one tiny thing. You're not bulletproof," Jack says.

Marius comes to my side. "It's too dangerous."

146

"You're staying put, Sela," Una says.

I dig my hand into my hip. "Then who has a better plan?"

We take fire once more, and my chest tightens. Una moves the vessel away, but we're clipped, and another two sensors turn red.

"How is the *Raptor* doing?" I ask.

"Let's find out," Una says, accelerating the *Scylla* through the water. For a moment, we're able to escape the targeting system of the two Syndicate vessels, but I doubt that will be for long.

Sirens and blinking lights erupt from the station. Una flips switches and taps several buttons on her console. Nothing changes. The sound grates on my ears and I can barely think.

"What's happening?" Pearl screams.

"We're going down," Jack says.

"We're not going down," Una cuts in. "Not if I can help it."

"Should we send a distress beacon?" I ask her. "At least then Atlantis will know we need more help."

"*Is* there more help?" Jack asks.

Flickering lights up ahead signal that the *Raptor* has lost electronics. Ignoring Jack, I grab the comm again and try to radio them.

As Una dodges the Syndicate torpedoes, there's no response from the *Raptor.* I have the urge to open the compression chamber myself, but we're moving too much for that to be safe for anyone.

Besides, Una can't lose her focus, and if I go out there, she will.

I race to the window. As we bob and weave, avoiding the Syndicate vessels, glimpses of the *Raptor* appear through the window. They're not in front of the comm tower anymore.

Una straightens the vessel, giving us a full view of the *Raptor*. They're sinking.

And to make matters worse, one of the Syndicate vessels is now back in formation, ahead of the *Raptor* and the ship's pathetic attempts to save the comm tower.

The *Scylla* dips and I plant my legs firmly as we drop. Marius stumbles, but I reach out, steadying him before he falls.

"This is stupid," Jack snarls. "I hate being stuck in this tin can when I could tear them apart with my hands!"

A retort falls from my lips as something darts out from one of the Syndicate vessels. The *Raptor* is still close enough to the comm tower that the Syndicate won't risk their mission by taking them down.

My heartbeat thrashes in my ears.

"Wait, what is that?" Jack asks, pressing his hands to the glass. He leans closer, and I instinctively do the same.

The launched torpedo moves away from the *Raptor* and circles around, crashing into the firing Syndicate vessel. The vessel nosedives toward the ocean floor.

It's not a torpedo; it's something else.

"Una, get us closer," I order, trying to keep the tremble out of my voice. I want to believe that what I'm seeing is true.

Una moves us toward the *Raptor* as something blurs across the water, streaking toward the falling Syndicate vessel.

The blur moves so quickly that I can't quite make out the shape. The object moves fast—fast like how I am in the water. It looks as if it's about to crash into us when it veers upward.

"Follow it!" I call to Una.

She turns the *Scylla* around just as the blur takes out the Syndicate vessel that had targeted us since our arrival. A hole rips through the front of the Syndicate vessel.

"Now's our chance," I say to Una. "Can you bring everything back online?"

"Working on it," she says. "We took some hard hits in case you didn't notice."

I ignore her snark and focus on what's unfolding in front of us. It's an even match now that whatever is out there has joined our side.

I rush over to Una and grab the comm again to radio the *Raptor*, but the captain still doesn't respond. Una manages to turn off the warning sirens, and a ringing settles in my ears.

"It's going after the vessel closest to the *Raptor*," Jack says. "We should take on the other ship."

"Do we have enough firepower?" I ask Una.

"We're going to find out now, aren't we?" she says. We're back in the fight, and my skin tingles with anticipation.

Una fires two consecutive torpedoes into the disabled Syndicate vessel. That's all it takes.

She shoots once more for good measure before turning toward the last Syndicate vessel. It's putting all its firepower against the blur, but the ship's too small and quick.

The *Scylla* straightens out in front of the Syndicate vessel. Our ship has nowhere to go. I peer through the front window and see the outline of their crew across the way.

"Fire," I say through gritted teeth.

Una presses the button and, seconds later, the vessel explodes, bursting with large plumes of heated exhaust that is quickly swallowed by water.

"Incoming," Una says. Her fingers hover over the station as the blur comes toward us.

"Father?" Marius chokes out.

Thacher floats in front of the window, staring at his son. The serum has reduced the scaly look of Marius's father, but he's still not back to the way we remember. He points upward as he reveals jagged sharp teeth. Is he smiling? Then he tilts his head back before swimming toward the surface.

Jack slowly turns around, arching his eyebrows. "You all saw that right?"

"He saved us," Pearl says.

Nyx flitters closer to Jack, her eyes glowing yellow.

Marius's eyes are wide and glossy. "Bring the *Scylla* to the surface."

"Is Atlantis safe?" I ask Una. As much as I want Marius to reunite with his father, I must protect my home too.

"I don't detect any more Syndicate vessels in the vicinity," Una says.

Walking over to Marius, I take his hand in mine. "Let's go then."

Una brings us to the surface and Marius sprints toward the upper hatch. I'm on his heels, and so are Jack and Pearl—Nyx hovering close behind.

As soon as we get to the exit, Una opens the hatch and Marius is the first outside. The salty scent of the water fills me as I come out next.

The *Echelon* floats nearby, and I'm finally able to let out a full breath.

"Is that . . . Ethan?" Pearl asks, shielding her eyes from the blazing sun above.

I narrow my gaze. Ethan stands on the deck of the *Echelon*, next to a soaking wet Thacher, raising a hand to us in greeting.

CHAPTER 15

Sela

THE *ECHELON* BOBS in the distance. The movement of the waves rocks the *Scylla*, and I have the urge to jump into the water and swim over. I can't believe that Thacher saved us. The serum must have cleared his mind, but I need to know for sure.

I glance at Marius. He shields his eyes with his hand, almost as if he still doesn't believe it either. "I want to see him."

"OK," I say.

A few minutes later, a small boat with Ethan at the controls, makes its way in our direction.

I turn to Una. "You good here? We're going to check on Thacher."

Una nods once. "As long as the Syndicate stays away for a little while, we're fine."

No doubt Nerissa has already been informed about what went down. The Syndicate was very close to recapturing control of Atlantis but, because of Thacher, we won this battle. The war is yet to come, but the scales will tip in our favor if Thacher is on our side.

"We won't be gone long," I say.

"We're sticking with Una," Jack says, pulling Pearl against his side. "We'll stay to man the *Scylla*."

"Let's go," I say to Marius, taking his hand in mine.

"What happened down there?" Ethan asks once we board the boat. He glances at Jack who shakes his head.

Ethan slides a glance at me and Marius. "That bad?"

"Let's just say, it was a good thing that Thacher came when he did," I say.

"That all of you did," Marius adds.

Ethan turns the boat in the direction of the *Echelon*, and we take off.

"How did you know we were in trouble anyway?" I ask Ethan.

"After you all left for Atlantis," Ethan says. "Cook's crew told me how he had ordered them to follow. That was fine with me. I want to be where the action is, not held back and made to wait. We kept a safe distance for a while until we detected the Syndicate vessels."

For once, I'm glad for Cook's selfishness.

When we reach the *Echelon*, Marius is the first to disembark, and I'm right behind him. Onboard, the crew moves around like a well-oiled machine, even in the absence of her captain.

In the far corner of the deck, Thacher sits on a small stool, his head in his hands. He's much bigger than he seemed in the ocean. His head moves slowly from side to side.

The last time we saw him, he lay unconscious atop a bed that barely fit his massive frame.

Marius stops, taking his hand in mine. The shock of his father being alive after Jack supposedly killed him appears to still be sinking in. He squeezes my hand and then releases my fingers. Marius moves forward, one slow step at a time like he's approaching a dangerous crocodile instead of his father.

"Father?"

Thacher's head snaps up, startled like he hadn't heard us before now.

"Is everyone alright?" Thacher's voice sounds similar to the movement of gravel rolling over itself. The tone is much deeper than originally, but not quite as monstrous as it had been before we administered the serum.

"We're all fine," Marius says.

"Thanks to you," I say, and Marius gives me a half smile.

Thacher sighs.

Marius drops to his father's side. Instinctively, I move forward, wanting to protect Marius. But he puts a hand out to stop me.

I clasp my hands together and filter all my nervous energy into my fingers. For once, I'm completely helpless. I know Thacher isn't a monster by choice, but I can't get the images out of my head from when he ripped apart the crew members and launched their disfigured bodies into the water. I doubt he can escape the horrifying images, either.

"I'm sorry for what I've done," Thacher says. "I understand why they all fear me. I couldn't stand by and allow the Syndicate to destroy anything else."

I see him through the mask of Nerissa's treatments. He's not the inhuman creature that attacked the *Echelon* under her orders, but he's not entirely himself yet. I wonder if another round of the serum would help? Or if there is any hope of getting another dose before Nerissa wants him back?

I step forward. "You helped us. We're so thankful for that."

He hangs his head again. "It doesn't make up for what I did before. To those men."

Marius kneels in front of his father. "It's not your fault."

"I had no idea who you were," Thacher continues with a faraway gaze. "I was a mindless minion for Nerissa." His lip curls with her name. "I'm so sorry."

Marius takes his hand. "I know what it feels like to be one of her experiments."

Thacher snorts, sounding more animalistic than human. "But even before this, I knew what she was doing. I helped her." He holds out his massive hands in front of him. "Enhancing us for survival is one thing, but her mission goes beyond that. Her control is unforgivable. I see that now."

His glossy eyes lift to mine and an ache pinches at my chest.

"What happened to you and Jack, as children . . ." He draws in a ragged breath. "Now I understand what that feels like. Something so out of your control—something unwanted—" his voice chokes off.

Marius chews on his bottom lip, biting back the emotion.

"We all did things we regret." This time, it's me who can't look him in the eyes. I had almost killed him during my escape from Nerissa.

"Don't," Thacher says. "You kids did what you needed to. I understand that now too."

My skin prickles and waves of tingles shoot up my arms and latch onto my spine. Thacher is alive, I shouldn't feel the swelling of guilt in my stomach. Yet, the unforgiving emotions swirl through my insides like ink from an octopus.

I walk over and stand beside him, touching his shoulder. He tilts his head in my direction. "The only one to blame for all of this is Nerissa. Now, all we can do is work together to stop her."

Thacher nods.

With that said, I have the urge to check on Atlantis. I want to know how many survivors there were and how much damage our forces incurred. I have no idea what Nerissa's planning next, but I want to stay as far ahead of her as possible.

"I'll be back soon," I say. "You two should have some time together."

Marius stands and takes my hands. "Thank you."

I kiss him on the cheek as my own cheeks flame. I don't know if Thacher knows about us but, if he didn't before, he does now.

Crossing the deck, I glance back at Marius and his father, looking over the ocean together. I hope Thacher eventually finds the strength to forgive himself.

As I climb the stairs to the bridge, my hands clench and unclench. Whatever repairs are needed on the *Scylla*, I worry they'll take too long to fix. We don't have a lot of help if Nerissa attacks again.

Two bearded, burly crew members are working on the bridge when I arrive. If I knew their names, I doubt I would still be able to tell them apart. Neither glances at me.

"Can I use this?" I ask, grabbing the comm.

"Make it quick," one says. "We have to keep the line clear."

I turn away and press a few buttons to sync up with the *Scylla*. "Una? Jack? It's Sela, you copy?" I release the comm and wait as the static sound fills the room.

"Sela," Una says over the line.

"How are the repairs coming?" I ask.

"Coming," she says. "Nerissa hit us pretty hard, but nothing substantial has been—" her voice cuts off, and I wait a few seconds before she returns. "Sorry, that drone got a little too excited. How are things there?"

I notice the burly beards leaning closer in my direction. Nothing I say will be new information, but the pirates seem to enjoy sticking their noses where they don't belong.

"Everything is fine. The serum worked well for Thacher. I wonder if we can make more?"

"That might have to wait for now," Una says.

I grit my teeth. "I know, just a thought."

"So," Jack's voice comes through the speakers. "He's not reptilian anymore?"

I roll my eyes. "Not as much."

"Does he remember almost killing us?" he asks.

I glance at the crew members across the way. Both of their jaws are set, apparently waiting for my answer.

"He remembers," I say.

"Good," Jack replies.

Before I can utter another word, Ethan appears across the bridge. His eyes are wild, and his breaths come hard and fast. He plants himself between the two pirates and me.

"What's wrong?" I ask.

"Over there." He points.

In the distance, a fleet of about a dozen vessels approach. I cradle the comm in my hand and press the button. "Una."

"I see them," she says.

"What do we do?" Ethan asks. "We don't have enough manpower to fight them off. Not with this ship and the *Scylla*."

"Calm down, boy," one of the pirates says.

Ethan's eyes narrow into slits.

My mind is a flurry of possibilities, but all end in our demise. Without Cook or Watts on board, the crew looks to me to decide. I debate on finding Marius to ask what he thinks, but there isn't time. The ships are closing in fast, and we are severely outnumbered.

Nerissa must not be taking chances anymore. By sending her fleet after us, she wants to take us down—for good. The weight of defeat sinks my shoulders, uncommon for me. My heart slows enough that each beat pounds in my head.

"What's that?" one of the pirates asks.

We clump together against the window as Papa's sleek, pearly-white warship emerges from the sea. It's double the size of the *Echelon* and far more advanced. I don't remember the last time I saw the vessel in commission.

A lightness fills my chest as several other similar, yet smaller, vessels pop up next to the warship, like surfacing whales. While the numbers aren't on our side, with Papa's ship and the *Echelon*, we do have some serious firepower.

Papa's voice crackles out of the speakers. "Sela, pick up the comm."

I rush across the bridge and grab it, ignoring the looks from the crew. "What have you heard?"

"We're going to end this," Papa says. "Atlantis is not for Nerissa's control."

"We're with you," I say.

The line goes dark, and I step forward to the farthest part of the bridge. If there is ever a time to be scared, now would be it.

"Prepare the cannons," I growl.

CHAPTER 16

Jack

THE SECOND THE Syndicate vessels come into view along the horizon line, Una's hands nearly blur across the operations deck in preparation for the battle to come.

"What's that?" I point to the radar. A large dot sits behind us on the screen, but Una doesn't seem fazed.

"Tritus's warship," she mumbles.

"Warship?" Pearl asks. "Are we doing this again so soon?"

"It's the perfect time to strike," Una says, and Pearl's eyes widen. "It's what I'd do if I were Nerissa."

I lick my lips. She's not helping Pearl feel any better and, admittedly, me neither. "What should I do?"

Una looks through the front window as the Atlantis vessels move toward the Syndicate. "I need everyone to stay calm and let me work."

Pearl's hand slips into mine. Once again, I regret not leaving her at Atlantis. At least there, she wouldn't be in the middle of a battle. Pearl is not made for this sort of thing. Sometimes I wish I weren't either. But it's way too late for that.

The Syndicate vessels position themselves in an attack formation. There are twice as many as there are Atlantis vessels, and they surround our side almost immediately. Two Atlantis vessels are taken down by heavy cannon fire and start to sink. Dark smoke dissipates as the boats drop to the ocean floor.

Una mutters a curse under her breath, and Pearl clamps her free hand over her mouth. I give the other one a squeeze.

Nyx comes down from her spot on the shelf and buzzes near my ear. I swat her away. She only wants to help, but I can't think straight.

A rumbling under our feet catches my attention as Tritus's ship appears next to ours. Canon fire booms, shaking our ship as Tritus attacks. Two Syndicate vessels are taken down by his vessel's fire. But it's not enough. They still outnumber us.

"I'm moving in," Una says.

"The Tritus warship is bigger than the Syndicate. If we go out there, we're only going to be in the way," I argue, inwardly cringing. If Pearl wasn't here, I would be all for fighting.

"We can't sit here and allow them to take down all of the Atlantis vessels," Pearl says, even though her hands are shaking.

"Looks like your girl is braver than you." Una smirks as a blip appears on the radar, emerging from the clump of Syndicate vessels. Una grunts as she navigates through the water, but the red dot comes at us fast. The *Scylla* shudders after impact. Another hit comes immediately.

"We're in firing range," Una says guiding the vessel off their radar radius. She swoops back in from another angle.

An object appears in the water in front of us, and I brace myself for impact. But it doesn't appear on the radar. Out the window, Sela's red hair swirls around her as she treads water before she dives under the surface again.

The only advantage we have against Nerissa is her experimentation. It's how I'm going to keep Pearl safe.

"I'm going out there," I say and signal to Nyx. She zips down to me and rests on my shoulder.

Pearl falls into my arms and a lump forms in my throat.

"Please be safe," she pleads.

I squeeze her against me, my body screaming not to let go.

Pearl moves away first and stands next to Una. "Tell me what I need to do."

I know the *Scylla* needs at least two people to man during battle, but that doesn't make leaving any easier.

Pearl tosses a look over her shoulder, and a smile touches her lips. "I'll be fine, Jack. Go get 'em."

I turn on my heel and sprint from the room. Nyx keeps up with me. The moment we reach the top hatch, I fling it open and fly up. Hovering above, I secure the lock before jetting up into the open sky. The rush of air over my skin sends a surge of electricity through me.

High above the battle, I'm able to view all the players. The *Echelon* hangs back, unloading round after round from their cannons. They won't be able to take too many hits from the Syndicate, so their position makes sense. The *Scylla* is between the warship and the Syndicate but gaining speed. At least with my help from the sky, maybe this fight can end sooner rather than later.

Nyx chirps from my side, and I spot one of the Syndicate vessels veering off course toward the *Scylla*.

"Nope, not happening," I mutter and shoot toward the ship.

Bursting up through the crisp air, I fly out of sight until I'm on top, then lower myself, hovering in front of the vessel's expansive bridge. A flurry of men scurry behind a span of glass windows and point weapons at me. No doubt, Nerissa wants her precious experiment back. But they'll have to catch me first.

Shooting up into the sky, the intense pull of gravity fades. Their cannons follow my path. So predictable. Once I'm beyond their targeting range, I fly toward Tritus's warship. Within seconds, Tritus opens fire on the vessel, sinking them.

Two more Syndicate vessels fall. Sela is doing her job well. Now, it's my turn to keep up.

Soaring down fast, I land hard on a smaller gunboat. The hull buckles and groans under my feet, leaving a large dent. Nyx reaches my sides and starts blasting at the hull's weak points. Sparks fly as she disables the electrical systems. The boat tries to veer off to shake me, but I dig my hands into a line of rivets and tear a large panel back.

Two men look up in shock as I drop in from the opening I just made. They have no time to draw their weapons. I backhand one into the control deck. Alarms blare. The second crewman lunges at me, but I drive my clenched fist into his gut. The Syndicate man falls to the floor, lifeless. With no time to waste, I set the boat to auto-destruct and lift off and out. Nyx follows me up, and we look down just in time to see the gunboat burst into white-hot flames.

Turning, I watch Tritus's warship hammer another Syndicate vessel with pulse cannons. The ship stands no chance as it cracks in half and sinks.

There's only one Syndicate vessel left. I expect, any minute, that they'll throw up a white flag or we'll sink their ship to the bottom of the ocean. Either way, we've won.

The thought compels me closer to the surface of the water. Knowing Pearl is safe draws me closer to the *Scylla*.

The sound of a cannon cuts through the sky and a breath whooshes out of me.

I expect to see the Syndicate vessel fall but, instead, my worst nightmare comes to life.

The *Scylla* turns at an unnatural angle, fire raging from its white hull. The ship sinks below the water.

"No!" I scream.

Within seconds, I'm hovering in the air where the *Scylla* went down. I glare at the water near my feet, expecting Pearl and Una to surface at any moment. Out of the corner of my eye, I see Sela swimming over. She pops up just below me.

"They shot the *Scylla* down." My words muddle in my ears as my breathing echoes in my head.

Sela's eyes widen in panic. Without a word, she dips below the surface. I want to follow, but I can't swim like her, and my abilities are practically nonexistent in the water.

I count the seconds in my head as the water blurs in front of me. Pearl has to be safe. All of this isn't for nothing. I stare at the waves, expecting the three to come up at any moment. But the seconds stretch on.

Without any other options, I fly upward and then dive into the water. With the momentum, I might be able to get to the *Scylla* to rescue Pearl.

The moment I dip my head under the water, a rippling explosion rockets me out again. I draw in the biggest breath I can muster, enough for my lungs to burn, and dive under once more. Sela needs my help. She can't swim to safety with both Una and Pearl. I know that she'll try to save her Sister first, as I'd do the same for Pearl.

Visibility limited, I keep pushing, even though my muscles ache as the weight of the ocean pushes on every inch of me.

A streak of red appears in my vision as Sela shoots to the surface. There's someone in her arms, and I use whatever strength I have left and follow her upward.

The moment I break through, I inhale a sharp breath, filling my lungs with the salty air. Sela bobs in the water, and I swim over to her. Her hair conceals the person in her arms.

She turns to me, and I see Pearl's face lifted to the sky. I choke out a breath.

"Take her, now!" Sela screams and shoves Pearl into my arms. Immediately, Sela plunges back into the water.

I jostle Pearl. "Pearl. Wake up." I tilt my head toward her. She's breathing—barely. She needs help. Nyx flits around my head, her eyes rotating between all the colored lights.

"She's going to be fine," I say aloud, entirely for my benefit as I scan the ocean. The *Echelon* is the closest vessel. I somehow manage to launch out of the water and head in that direction.

The second I land on deck, several crew members glance my way. I run past them, keeping Pearl close to my chest, so I don't damage her more than she already is.

"Keep breathing, Pearl. Stay alive. I'm going to get you some help."

Her eyes don't open.

The vessel-sized lump in my throat grows as I descend to the lower deck. With Thacher out of the med bay, there's probably a place for Pearl.

I burst into the room and spot a medic sitting by a computer. "Help her."

He scrambles to his feet. He's thin yet tall form towers over me. The gold hoop in his ear glints under the light. "Put her on the bed."

I do as he says, but I don't let go of Pearl's hand as he inspects her. The only sign of life is her chest rising ever so slightly.

"She was in one of the vessels taken down," I say and bite my lip.

Someone darkens the doorway, and I turn to see Ethan. "Jack. We need you on the bridge."

I shake my head. "I'm staying with Pearl."

Ethan grits his teeth. "You're going to want to see this."

"There's nothing you can do here," the crew member says. "She's in good hands. I promise."

I hesitate, tracing the lines of her face with my eyes.

"Jack," Ethan urges.

"I know," I growl. I kiss her hand and then bolt from my chair and follow Ethan toward the main deck. "This better be important."

"It is," Ethan says. "A game-changer for sure."

The Syndicate vessels were taken out. There's no way Nerissa replenished her fleet that quickly.

Once I reach the deck, I look around, expecting to see more Syndicate vessels. Instead, every single crew member stares into the sky.

The rumbling is the first thing I hear as I follow their attention. I have no idea why they're looking at the clouds until one sticks out as a little too sharp. It's not a cloud. My body tenses as I take in the massive flying vessel with the Syndicate logo painted on the side coming toward us. Tritus's warship is miniature compared to that thing.

"As I said," Ethan says.

"Game-changer," I finish for him. While we had our sights on the water, Nerissa reached higher, somehow moving upward instead of below.

We head over to the bridge where several crew members stand there, stunned at the new development.

Nyx rests on my shoulder and cuddles close to my neck. I feel for her, wishing I could burrow myself in a safe place. While Nerissa is alive, nowhere is safe.

A young man approaches me with a comm device. "Tritus is asking for you."

I take the device from him. "Flynn, here."

"I need you to fly over our ship," Tritus booms over the line.

Everything I hold dear to me is on the *Echelon*. Once again, I'm leaving Pearl behind. But there isn't a safer place for her. The only person who keeps putting her in danger is me.

Sela saved Pearl, the least I can do is help her father.

I turn to Ethan. "I'm going."

Ethan nods. "I'll stay with Pearl."

I squeeze his shoulder. "Thanks."

Nyx rises into the air and buzzes around my head.

"You stay here too," I say to her. "Watch the horizon for more vessels."

Her eyes burn blue, but I move away from her and press the button on the side of the device. "On my way."

I'm in the air again. The massive vessel in the distance hovers over the water. I wonder what this Syndicate ship is waiting for. The craft could easily take us all out. Nerissa needs something—probably the only reason she hasn't destroyed us yet. A shiver rolls up my spine, but I focus on the warship and speed up, wanting to get back to Pearl as soon as possible.

On Tritus's ship, several decks are separated by tall comm towers. I land on the closest deck and wait for Tritus to arrive. The vessel is a ghost town. Was calling me truly an emergency?

A stinging, sharp pain digs into my neck. The world around me tilts, and my face smacks onto the deck. My vision fills with dark spots, and I try to get up, but I can't.

"Whaaa—?" a groan escapes my lips.

A pair of boots approach me. I don't even have the strength to lift my gaze.

A whirring sound comes near, too, and then something is lifting me. First, I notice the long rod, and then I come face-to-face with Tritus.

"It has to be you," he says. "Then this will all be over."

I have no idea what he's talking about.

Hands are all over my body as I'm lifted onto something hard. I try to stay conscious. Whatever he had hit me with stung badly. My stomach swoops as something pulls me into the sky. He can't even look me in the eye, but I try to focus and stay awake.

A glass door closes in front of me, and I blink. When I open my eyes, I'm much higher in the sky. I already know where I'm going and feel the sinking sensation of betrayal coil through my body. The *Echelon* gets farther and farther away. I blink away the heat behind my eyes. At least, Pearl will be OK.

I notice movement in the air between the *Echelon* and me. Nyx's blinking colors are a beacon.

Stay, I try and get the word out, but my command repeats in my head only. She gets closer, and she tries so hard. I blink, and the next thing I see is her—in a million pieces—plummeting toward the water.

CHAPTER 17

Sela

"NO!" MY SCREAM is muffled by the water and goes nowhere.

I claw at the surface of the mangled hull now resting on the ocean floor, the metal shredding the skin on my fingers. I can't lose another Sister to Nerissa.

I frantically swim around the vessel searching for the scorched opening in the hull that I pulled Pearl from. But the breach is now resting face-down on the bottom. My mind carousels trying to come up with a solution—any solution that saves Una. Once more, I dart around to search the metal surface and, when I find nothing that will get me inside, I run my fingers through my hair in desperation. I don't have Jack's strength. There's no way I can pry open the thick composite outer hull. Water has filled every inch inside by now. I'm the only one of us that can survive underwater that long.

My tears mix with the seawaters. And for a wild heartbeat, I think I see Una bobbing in the distance, safe and sound. But as quickly as she came, she's gone. An illusion.

"She's gone," I mutter, my voice sounds deep inside my head. An echo.

My stomach clenches with the knowledge she's dead and if I don't get up top my other friends may die, too. With one final glance at the *Scylla*, I turn and zip up toward the surface, bursting through.

Overhead, Jack flies in the direction of Papa's warship. Where's he going? I take in the massive vessel floating above us. The image of the Syndicate logo burns in my vision. This is Nerissa's plan? Taking over the sky? I shake off all my questions. None of them matter. I just need to find Jack and do whatever I can to make Una's sacrifice worth something—anything.

I dive under the surface, unable to look back. Streams of cool water rush past my body as I tear through the ocean. I reach the *Echelon* quickly. Making my way to the port side's ladder, I scale the rusted metal rungs two at a time, jump over the railing, and then storm across the deck.

In a sea of familiar faces, I look for Ethan. He'll know what's going on. Again, the tears burn in my eyes, but I wipe them away with the back of my hand. A crippling ache blooms in my chest, and I clench my teeth, willing the pain away.

Pearl appears from below decks, staggering in my direction. Her eyes and hair are wild, looking more like a sea creature than Jack's love. I let out a breath. At least she's OK.

A question hangs on my lips, but before I'm able to ask, Pearl cuts me off. "What's happening? Where's Jack?"

"I just got here," I say, turning toward Papa's ship. "But I saw Jack flying over there. Toward the warship."

Pearl shakes her head furiously. "What? By himself? Why?"

I glance around, looking for someone to give us answers. Ethan is on the bridge, and as I take one step toward him, Pearl clutches my arm.

"Wait." Her voice is hoarse and much deeper than I've ever heard.

Something dark and small hovers above Papa's ship, and I narrow my eyes to get a better look. "Jack is being loaded on that thing."

"Where are they taking him?" Pearl begs.

"I'll give you one guess," I say as the small craft lifts toward the floating vessel, now with Jack onboard.

A buzzing sound fills my ears. For a second, I think the *Echelon* is prepping to attack Papa's warship. But I quickly realize it's Nyx, going after Jack. Her little body flies off the deck faster than I've ever seen. She's loyal; I'll give her that.

"No!" I yell. "Get back here, Nyx!"

Ethan sprints over to us. "Sela. I just saw—"

Nyx's small frame explodes in midair, making us flinch back.

I clamp a hand over my mouth just as Pearl screams Jack's name. Ethan curses under his breath.

Nyx is gone. Just like that.

And so is Jack.

I whirl to Ethan. "Tell me everything."

Ethan pants, his eyes on the sky. "Your father—he radioed over to us and asked Jack to fly over there. I didn't think—"

"You didn't think what?" Pearl asks.

Ethan lifts his eyes to mine. "I thought he was going over for some sort of covert conversation off the comms. I—I didn't . . ."

I track the small vessel docking inside a port on Nerissa's craft.

"This doesn't make sense. Why would Papa allow them to take Jack? No. There must be something else going on."

"Something happened on that ship just after Jack flew over there," Ethan says.

"I'm going to find out," I say, as a swirl of unease moves through me.

No one else is going to get hurt because of me. My chest tightens, and I stop to catch my breath. Una and Derya's faces flood my vision. Both died because of my decisions.

I'm not going to let that happen to Jack. If Papa has something to do with it, I'll never forgive myself.

"I'm going with you," Marius says, coming up from behind me. I twist and find Thacher next to him, but he says nothing.

"Me too," Pearl says, her red-rimmed eyes boring into mine.

Ethan is by her side, and he nods once. "I'll stay here. I'll try to gather intel on that thing up there."

"I'll go too," Thacher says in a deep voice.

"Father, stay here," Marius insists. "I need people here I can trust if things go south."

"Let's not waste any more time then," I say and walk over to the railing. I climb up and leap into the water. They can catch up with me. There isn't time to waste.

The water soothes the heat from my body. How did my life turn into this mess in such a short amount of time? I keep close to the surface, so Marius and Pearl know where I am.

Deep guilt fills me as I swim over where the *Scylla* went down. I grabbed Pearl first, thinking she was Una. I'll never tell Jack that, but I'm sure he knows what I would do.

Reality crashes through me. Una is dead. A flurry of bubbles swirls around me as I let out a ragged breath.

By the time I reach the surface, Marius and Pearl have nearly caught up to me in a smaller boat. Marius is at the controls while Pearl stands next to him, their eyes on Papa's ship.

I shoot ahead and reach the vessel first. I need to find out what happened before Pearl goes berserk on Papa. There's no way that Papa would allow Nerissa to take Jack. That's not who he is anymore. The sight of the white, smooth hull breaks me from my anguished thoughts. The skiff from the *Echelon* drifts up and a large hatch opens from the side of the hull, just out of the water. It retracts in and I climb up before Marius and Pearl dock their craft.

Ignoring Papa's crew, I make my way through the lower levels and reach the main deck. I expect the worst but, instead, I find Papa standing there, unharmed, and his eyes lifted to the sky.

"Papa." I rush to his side. I look him up and down and breathe a sigh of relief. It's the first time I've taken a deep breath since leaving Una to the sea. "What happened? Did they try and hurt you?"

He looks at me, his thick eyebrows furrowed.

I drop my head down. "I saw the Syndicate take Jack."

Papa squeezes his eyes shut.

"He set Jack up, didn't he?" Marius asks, walking up from the other side of the deck. He and Pearl both have similar versions of disgust across their faces.

"Papa, tell them that's not true."

"I did," Papa says, lifting his chin. "It was the only way."

Pearl braces herself against Marius, unable to take in what she's hearing. "After all he's been through, you sent him back to her? Why?"

"It was the only way to keep Atlantis and Sela safe," Papa says. "Nerissa threatened to destroy Atlantis and take you both for her future plans. I saved you, Sela."

"By sacrificing my friend?" I shriek.

Papa nods. "I won't let her have you again."

Pearl sobs and her knees buckle, but Marius grabs her by the waist before she hits the floor.

There had to be another way. My mind swirls. Papa wasn't thinking straight when he made that deal with Nerissa. By getting Jack, she can create the perfect human to survive in her new world.

My attention pulls to Cook and Watts walking along the deck toward us, almost as if they don't have a care in the world.

"Did you know?" Marius demands. I hiccup back a sob. As much as he and Jack aren't the best of friends, even *he* knows this is wrong.

Their faces speak volumes before either utter a single word.

"They were involved in the conversation as well," Papa says.

Cook adjusts his glasses over the bridge of his nose. "It's the reason we came to Atlantis. We had to make a deal, or we would lose everything."

"All of you traded one innocent person to keep your vessels?" Marius asks with a snort of disdain.

Cook crosses his arms. "Not just the *Echelon* but all of my men. I must protect them as well. And Jack isn't all that *innocent.*"

Marius launches himself at Cook. Their bodies crash to the ground, and Pearl leaps away from the scuffle. Cook cries out for Watts as Marius lifts his fist. Watts grabs onto Marius's arm and pulls back before the punch connects with Cook's cheek. With much effort, Watts manages to get Marius off Cook, and the little man scrambles away from the enhanced threat.

Marius's chest heaves and his teeth flash at his friend. Or possibly ex-friend now.

"Marius, enough," I say, and that gets his attention. "This is wasting time. We need to get onto that ship and get Jack before it's too late."

He backs up, panting. "How do you think we can get up there?"

"We have to try. Jack would do the same for any of us."

Marius clenches his jaw before reaching into his pocket and retrieving a comm. He presses the button to speak. "Father."

"Marius." Thacher's voice sounds. "I'm here."

Marius looks right at me before turning to Cook, a combination of grief and anger flushing his skin. "Take command of the *Echelon*. Captain Cook is no longer worthy of the title."

"You can't do that," Cook snarls.

Marius lifts his finger off the device. "I just did."

"You're a fool," Cook growls. "Nerissa is too powerful."

Ignoring Cook, Marius glances over his shoulder at the *Echelon*. A crew member launches over the side of the vessel and crashes into the water. He resurfaces, angry, and swims in our direction.

"Nerissa doesn't expect us to go after Jack," I say. "Thanks to your trade, she probably thinks we're in this together." I narrow my eyes at Papa, wondering how I could have ever trusted him to do the right thing after how he betrayed all those innocent children and their families.

"Sela," Papa says, reaching for me.

I move away from him. I can't even look him in the eyes. "Don't try and stop us. If we don't do this now, Nerissa will only grow so powerful that no one will be able to protect Atlantis, or anywhere else for that matter."

Papa presses his lips together in a line so thin, they disappear under his beard. "I did this for you. So you could live, little minnow."

I glance at Papa's crew members. Between Marius and me, we could fight off most of them. But there isn't enough time for fighting. "I'm going whether you like it or not."

And I haven't been his little minnow since the day he let me go. He knows that now.

He swallows, "Go save Jack."

My heart breaks for him, but I don't let it show. He lost everything when we lost Mama. He doesn't want to lose me too. If I acknowledge those feelings, though? I'll never leave his side. And it's not my job to protect his feelings. The consequences of choosing for other families to know the gripping fear and pain of loss are his to own.

"I'll never let you take my ship," Cook says and rushes Pearl—the weakest target. But before he reaches her, Papa orders his men to hold Cook and Watts. Watts lunges, but three men take him to the floor, pointing a gun at his head. Cook stops and throws his hands in the air, giving up easily. The coward.

"Bring them below deck to cool off," Papa says.

"Marius," Thacher says through the comm. "The *Echelon* is in our command. How do you want to proceed?"

"We're on our way," Marius says and clicks off.

"I can't stay here," Pearl pleads.

I wave for Pearl to follow and the three of us dash down through the vessel to our craft. I grasp Marius's hand the entire way back to the *Echelon*. We're walking into danger, and we all know it.

Marius holds the throttle forward as far as possible and we skim on the water surface, wind nearly pushing us into the sea. I hold onto Pearl with my free hand and she offers a soft smile in return. Once we're safely on the *Echelon*, we race over to the bridge. Thacher and Ethan are at the helm, and the remaining crew members fall in line.

Thacher stands before his son and bows his head. "The vessel is yours, Captain."

Marius takes his father's hand, shakes it, and then pulls him into a brief embrace. Then he walks over to the controls. "Follow the flying vessel."

CHAPTER 18

Jack

A HAZY FOG shimmers on the edge of my vision as I walk the main corridor of the ship. I've been at this game for far too long, and my friends are going to make fun of me if I can't find at least one of them. Something moves out of the corner of my eye, and a slow smile spreads across my face.

The nearest alcove used to be a gift shop of some kind when this boat had shuttled people around the world on vacations. Since we colonized the ship, it's been repurposed into a storage room. We're not allowed in the storage spaces, but that's a part of the game.

It's not the first time we've played, and nine times out of ten, we end up in trouble. Not getting caught is part of the game. Which is probably why it's taken me so long to find *anyone. I get several side-eyes from the adults passing by. I don't need to wonder why.*

I move to the side. If whoever is behind the door sees me, then I'll lose the element of surprise, and that's my favorite part.

Holding my breath, I reach for the door handle as my heart slams in my chest. My fingers brush against the handle right as something hard falls onto my shoulder. Within seconds, I'm ripped away from the door, and I come face-to-face with someone new.

I quickly make up an excuse. "We're just playing. I wasn't going to take anything."

The man's mouth presses into a thin, white line as he holds me in place. He doesn't look like the protectors on the ship. He's in uniform, but not one I've seen before.

My stomach sinks, and I shake my head as his grip tightens.

"Honey, don't struggle." Mom's voice comes from behind the strange man.

The door behind me clicks open, and I see my friend, Ginny, peeking her head through. I slowly shake my head. I have no idea how much trouble I'm in, and I don't want her to be as well. We all cover for each other here, at least the kids do. If Mom is involved, then I know without a doubt that this is serious.

"What's going on?" I ask as two more uniformed men come into view.

Tears streak Mom's cheeks, and she's holding onto the crook of Dad's arm. Deep lines crease around his mouth.

My insides tremble, but I try to be strong for Mom. Anytime I get into trouble, she always smiles and shakes her head before ruffling my white-blond hair. "Kids will be kids," she's said too many times.

But with no smile or hair ruffling, I already know there's more to this. Something isn't right. And I don't want to go with these men.

"You have the others?" the man asks his friends.

The other two nod, their gazes barely reaching the man. Is this guy in charge or something? Who do they have, and why?

"This is a mistake," I say. "I won't be bad again, please." Even though I have no idea what I've done that's so horrible. Maybe if they see that I'm sorry, they won't take me. "I promise to be good!"

"Come on," he says, tugging me away from my parents and Ginny.

"No!" I scream and try to pull away from him. Somehow the other two end up behind me and, just as I come out of one's grip, I'm within the other's.

The shimmering fog in my periphery intensifies, as though connected to my racing heart. I struggle against them, but they're too strong. Three people hold my wiggling body and then lift me from the ground. Screams echo in my head, yet all I hear are Mom's sobs.

My eyes spring open. As I slam into the hazy present, the grip of Syndicate soldiers presses all around me. I rock my shoulders back and forth, but they barely move. The men show no emotion on their cold faces. I don't feel right when I take a breath and try to regroup. I must have been dreaming. My thoughts return to Tritus shocking me before the Syndicate took me. Thoughts of betrayal fill every corner of my mind. Tritus played me and that must have triggered the memory of when I was taken as a young child. Mom just stood there as Nerissa's men took me away all those years ago.

The events leading up to now come back slowly as if I'm watching the scene through someone else's eyes.

Tritus did this to me. To Nyx. The image of her small body exploding in midair replays in my mind. Once again, I struggle against my tight bindings. An ache settles in my wrists and shoulders.

I look around. The ceiling is incredibly high, maybe twenty feet. I'm in a large room, but other than the low, steady rumbling of the engines, I don't hear much. The way my head is held in place, I can't see much else either.

"Lift him up." Nerissa's voice turns my blood to ice. The contraption I'm strapped to starts to move, and the heat from before drains from my body.

There *is* someone else with me. A thin man in a lab coat. His sunken cheekbones make him look more like a corpse than a person. I shiver, wondering if Nerissa may have dabbled in more than experiments on the living.

He stops me at a strange angle. I'm almost in a standing position, but still somewhat laying down. Nerissa approaches me, a smirk dancing on her lips. I wish they had given me access to one of my hands, so that I could wipe the sneer off her face.

"I see you're working with Tritus again," I say.

Nerissa juts her lower lip out and shrugs. "Or he's working for me. His little daughter means everything to him. When you love someone that much, it makes you weak."

I think of Pearl. I'll do anything to keep her safe. Has that made me weak?

Nerissa pulls on the ends of her ponytail, widening her eyes and intensifying her heartless gaze. "As much as I would love to have you and Sela on my side, there's been a change of plans."

"Wonderful," I snap.

She stops next to me, close enough that I could grab her lab coat if I weren't bound to the table. But that little detail doesn't stop me from trying. My fingers curl toward her but, even with all my strength, I can only move a few centimeters.

I relax, holding onto my strength. For now.

"It *is* wonderful," she says, obviously not acknowledging the sarcasm in my tone. "You, Jack, are so valuable to my work. I allowed Sela and Atlantis to remain unharmed in exchange for you. I could take them down. But I want to avoid further loss and conflict. I'm positive with my recent advancement and your genetics, I'm able to surpass any need for the water and the creatures and habitats it contains."

The advancement she's talking about must be what she did to Thacher. He was as good as dead after I shot him. But I don't think she cares too much about him now. She's been too busy.

Searing white heat surges through me, and I buck against the harness surrounding me. I'm a lab rat again.

Nerissa doesn't flinch. She clearly thinks I won't be able to escape, but I'll find a way.

"What do you think of my new home?" she asks, holding her hands out on either side of her.

I glance around, finally getting a good look at the room. It's cavernous with several different stations throughout. Each has a computer and various pieces of equipment. A few of the Syndicate soldiers mill around the room, working on whatever nefarious projects she's assigned them.

"Cozy," I deride.

Nerissa's smile wavers. "How you've held onto that humor of yours surprises me. There's really nothing funny about what I plan for you."

I like getting under her skin. She expects me to roll over and take it from her, but she's wrong about that. Once I'm in the air again, she won't be able to catch me.

"Where did you find this hunk of junk?" I ask.

She shakes her head. "While the ship is not quite as advanced as Tritus's vessel, it gets the job done. I found the abandoned wreck in an old-world drifting shipyard I came across years ago. I never thought it would be much of anything, until I started tinkering, away from the main Syndicate. The fewer people who knew, the better."

"How clever of you," I say, gritting my teeth.

"I think so too." She raises an eyebrow. "That shipyard has been my secondary base of operations for some time. It's in far too much disrepair to live on though, that's why I sought out your precious Avalon."

"Which we took back," I say, reminding her of her failures.

Her eyes narrow. "Once Avalon was no longer an option, I knew it was the perfect time to bring out my reclaimed flying vessel. I hoped to have had a fleet in the water and air, but that's all forgotten now."

Because we took them down. Her experiments fought back, and she couldn't take it.

"The air is the future. The sky is mine for the taking." She opens her hand and indicates the large windows on the other side of the room. White fluffy clouds move past us, slowly, as if they don't have a care in the world. All while Nerissa claims the space as her own.

"Which is why you want me." My mouth dries up immediately. If she's able to create more like me, those in the water don't stand a chance.

"It's time for humanity to strive beyond the waters and rule the air."

"Your speech is all well and good, but if you think I'm going to help you, then you're preaching to the wrong audience."

She comes closer to me, enough so her breath moves across my face. Her lip curls in a snarl. "I don't need you. I need what's inside of you. If I had any thought of you helping me, you wouldn't be harnessed. I don't trust you, Jack. But you're going to help me, with or without your permission."

Rage fills me. I clench my fists.

Her cackling laughter echoes in my ears as she saunters over to the guy in the dark lab coat. "Prep him for stem cell extraction and testing."

He nods. Nerissa takes one more look at me before strolling across the room toward an open door.

I count eight other men in the room. Once I find a way out of the harness, I'm going for that door. I study the dilapidated guy, and he's hooking up a long needle to a clear plastic tube, one connected to a bag. If Nerissa doesn't need me, does she intend to take all my blood?

I can't let that happen. I'm going to get back to Pearl, no matter what.

"This won't hurt if you keep still," the guy says to me. His hands tremble slightly, and I know it's going to hurt no matter what. Flashes of previous experiments flood my mind. None were pleasant, and *all* of them hurt like hell.

He's aiming for my arm when an idea pops into my head. Using most of my strength, I turn my arm inward, blocking him from reaching my vein.

"Turn a little my way," he says.

I click my tongue. "I would if I could. These things are a little tight."

The end of the needle brushes against my skin, and I can't help but suck in a breath. I hope this idea works, or else it's going to hurt far worse than I had hoped.

The needle pokes me but doesn't break the skin.

The technician sighs and pulls back, dropping the needle onto a nearby table. He lifts a tablet and his fingers run across the screen. The harness around my right arm loosens.

This is it.

I don't move my arm. I want him to release me as much as possible before I strike.

Holding my breath, I wait until he touches my arm and turns it to the side. He's about to put the harness back into place when I crash my fist into the side of his head. He goes down like an anchor. His body smacks into the table with the needle, making a lot of noise. The Syndicate soldiers turn my way as I push with all my might. The harness cracks with the pressure, and I shimmy out, just as two other men approach me. I fly above them, feeling a surge of energy pulse through me.

I know I'll have a lot more to fight, so I reserve my strength and fly across the room through the door. I close it and turn the knob, hard enough to crush it.

At least I have a head start before they alert anyone to my escape.

As I navigate the maze of corridors, a plan forms in my mind. The ceilings are tall, which gives me an advantage. But soon enough, I come across six Syndicate guards who fire their weapons at the same time.

I shoot to the ground and dart around the guards, taking each one down. The guards fall on top of each other, scrambling to get up again. But I get away before they do.

At the end of one corridor, there's an opening to the sky. The only thing holding me back from Pearl is a door. I could easily escape and fight from the water. But Nerissa's aerial advantage is much more than what the *Echelon* and Tritus's warship can deal with. It's up to me to even the playing field.

I tear away from the door as several more Syndicate soldiers cut me off in the corridor. A woman with a buzzcut charges at me, a battle cry ripping from her. I dodge her strike and elbow her in the head, buckling her knees. Without a thought, I pick her up and toss her at the two guys a few feet back. Her limp body slams into the guards, forcing everyone into the back wall. None of them move now.

I need to find the engine room. If I can take down the ship, then Nerissa has nothing to her advantage. If she's given up on water travel, then I bet everything she has is on this air vessel. Destroying the ship destroys her.

I head deep into the belly of this vessel when a diagram on the wall catches my attention. A map. The engine room is at the end of the hallway. A rusted metal door stands before me. With a hard kick, I knock it down and take a step inside. Walls of flickering lights fill the space, connected by wires and tubes. Voices in the hallway ring out and I spring into action. I head for the setup closest to me and grab onto a fist-full of wires and rip them out. The wires snap, and their frayed edges spark against my skin.

I use all my strength to pull more from the other sections. I do as much damage as I can to ensure that this thing will never fly again.

I crash to the floor as the vessel pitches. Scrambling up, I grab onto another grouping of thick cabling and pull them free from their sockets. My breathing comes harder. I've been in near-death experiences before, but this one adds the extra pressure of saving everyone in the waters below. I know Sela will be upset with me for taking out Nerissa first, but she'll eventually get over it.

The vessel pitches again, nosediving toward the water. An intense alarm throbs in my enhanced eardrums. The sound is messing with my thoughts.

"Time for my exit," I say and hover over the ground. There's a door on the other side of the room. I fly in its direction, already feeling Pearl's hand in mine, when a blast of heat sears my skin. I can't hear anything other than ringing in my ears as I'm thrown against the wall. Blackness fills my vision as I crash to the floor.

CHAPTER 19

Sela

MY FINGERS DIG deeper into my palms with each second as we get closer to the flying vessel. Because of Papa, Nerissa has Jack once again. I wish I were on deck when Jack received the comm from Papa. I would have gone with him. Saved him.

Or she might have captured both of us.

No, Papa wouldn't have allowed it.

I try not to worry about how we're going to get into the vessel, once we get close enough. My best friend is probably strapped to a table—unconscious—or worse.

I shake the thought from my head. This is Jack. He's a survivor, like me and Thacher. Nerissa might have a twisted mind, but Jack is stronger than her. He'll find a way out.

"What's that?" Pearl brings my attention back to the present. She leans over the controls to look out at Nerissa's vessel.

Thick, black smoke plumes from the underbelly. Through the smoke, flickers of red and orange erupt like lightning.

My heart stills. We're too late. I glance at Marius. His mouth sets in a hard line.

Thacher stands behind us, wordless and focused on the scene ahead.

"I bet Jack did that," Ethan says with a smirk.

"What just happened?" Pearl asks. As if one of us might know.

I pat her arm. "Ethan might be right."

Pearl's entire body trembles. "How can you be so sure?"

I grit my teeth, wishing she would stop talking. I need to think. I scour the sky for Jack. If he sabotaged the vessel, where is he? Wouldn't he be on his way back down to us, ready to fight?

A breath catches in my throat.

"We need to move out of the way," Marius yells to his men.

Ethan, now Marius's first mate, responds immediately to his captain, and the *Echelon* veers to the left.

The nose of the flying vessel pitches downward and, within seconds, plummets into the water.

Pearl steps forward, hand cupped over her mouth. Her eyes are locked onto the chaos.

"Hold on!" I cry as the vessel crashes too close to our boat.

A few seconds later, a wave slams against the *Echelon*'s hull and the entire vessel shudders.

Pearl flies backward and Ethan grips her arm. Marius and I grab onto the control panel as the waves continue to crash into the boat. We were too close to the vessel. If it weren't for Marius directing us elsewhere, we could have capsized, causing bigger issues than we already have.

Once we're steady, Marius fires orders to the men to move the *Echelon* away from the crash site. There's too much wreckage, and we can't afford to damage the ship.

"We have to go out there," I say to Marius. "At least, I do. If Jack—" I glance at Pearl and shut my mouth.

"We need to take the skiff," Marius says.

Pearl perks up and crosses over to Marius. "I'm coming. I don't care what any of you say."

I don't argue with her. If Marius was on that vessel, I'd say the same thing.

"I'm coming too," Thacher says. "I'm of better use over there."

Marius draws in a deep breath. "Ethan, can you keep things running on the *Echelon*?"

"Of course," Ethan says with a snort.

Marius nods and walks over to the two crew members, giving them orders to listen to Ethan in his absence.

"Come on," I say to Pearl.

When we reach the side of the *Echelon*, Thacher loosens the skiff from the railing. Marius and I help Pearl inside. Smoke billows from the shattered windows of Nerissa's fallen vessel. I cross my fingers and pray that Ethan was right. Jack has to be the one who took the ship down.

Once they're inside, I dive into the water. With the momentary reprieve from the chaos of the surface, my mind clears. As much as I want to mourn Una and be angry with Papa, Jack is the only face that fills my mind. I can't let him die for nothing, for Father's betrayal, and Una's loss.

I break through the surface as the boat rocks in the water next to me.

Thacher dives. Even though he's a massive guy, he barely makes a splash.

Marius starts the engine at the back of the skiff.

The water invigorates me, and I glance at Nerissa's vessel. It would be easy enough to swim over and get on board before this boat does.

"Sela," Marius says with a warning in his voice.

I turn. "What?"

"I know what you're thinking. You're not going off on your own. We're in this together, OK?"

I hate that Marius knows what I'm thinking. My enhancements were made for a rescue mission like this. I'm so much faster than the boat. If I can get ahead of them, then I can start looking for Jack.

"Marius is right," Thacher says to me. "We don't know what's in that water. There could be exposed wires or toxic chemicals spilling into the ocean."

"All right," I say and climb onto the small boat.

Thacher's lumbering body rocks us, nearly knocking us all off the skiff as he takes a seat at the back. The boat settles and we're good to go.

Marius pushes the throttle forward and the torque lifts us in the front, raising even farther up as we jolt along the water surface toward the downed vessel. My fingers dig into my seat's armrests.

"We should go around the side," Marius shouts through the wind. "Over there."

Syndicate soldiers pour out of an escape hatch, jumping into the water. I suppose the Terran Sea is better than burning to death. Several row away on emergency boats, but their forces are seriously depleted. I wonder if Nerissa put all her men on the flying ship? Or if she has a large crew ready to blast the *Echelon*, as well as us, off into the distance while she keeps Jack for herself.

"There's another hatch, but it doesn't look like anyone is coming out," Marius says, breaking through my thoughts.

"What if it's blocked off, or there's a fire inside?" Pearl asks, her eyes widening to saucers.

"There's only one way to find out," Thacher says.

"We don't have a lot of time," Marius says, steering the boat toward the hatch. "It's going under faster than we thought." He shares a look with his father and then slides his gaze to me.

I pull a slow breath through my teeth. Jack is going to be fine. He has to be.

The skiff bumps against the side of the vessel, and Thacher grabs the bottom of the hatch, moving the boat closer.

Marius pulls the metal door open and it pops as the air pressure releases. Hot air rushes out, and we flinch, grimacing until the blast fades. With a nod, Marius steps in first, and I'm close behind him. Pearl and Thacher follow us. As much as I'm worried about Pearl, having Thacher and Marius with us eases my mind.

The darkness is interrupted by bursts of pulsing orange light from the alarm system. Inside the vessel is nothing but chaos. Syndicate soldiers run for the nearest exit, barely acknowledging our presence. We're on the end that isn't flooded yet, but sparks of electricity blink in the air around us. In one room to the left, a fire consumes all the furniture inside.

Thacher reaches inside the room to close the door.

"Hey, stop right there!" a soldier shouts from next to me.

I barely turn as his fist skids across my cheek. I turn, grab his arm and twist. He screams out in pain, and I kick him in the stomach and then toss him to the ground.

Marius has his pistol out in front of him. The three of us are enough, but more firepower can't hurt.

The corridors are dark now, only lit by the lights shorting out along the wall. They flicker, and some sputter out, as we walk deeper into the vessel.

We surround Pearl, and her chattering teeth overpower the sounds of the dying engines.

"Here's a map," Marius says, walking over to the wall.

I stand next to him, trying to find our location. Part of the map hangs loose from the wall. But a red dot marks where we are compared to all the outlined emergency exits.

"We have company," Thacher says.

Syndicate soldiers pour out of one side of the hallway. Some battered and bruised, but all have the same look of alarm on their faces.

"Stay here, Pearl," I say to her.

She backs against the wall as Marius, Thacher, and I walk toward the enemy. Two of them run off down another hallway—mere jellyfish who can't handle a fight.

Thacher grabs a Syndicate soldier in the front and wrestles for control of his weapon. Marius charges the next two, who are ready to fire at his father. Something tugs at my hair and twists, hard. I crash to the floor and look up, staring at a barrel of a gun.

The man wielding the weapon smiles.

I smile back as I kick my foot out and swipe to the side. He loses his balance, and his grip falters. I grab his arm and pull him down to my level. The gun slips from his hand, and I toss it away. I want to kill him, but I save the urge for Nerissa.

"Where's Jack?" I growl.

"Who?" he asks.

"The flying one," I say through gritted teeth.

"I have no idea," he cries out.

My fist connects with his jaw, and he shrieks. "Where. Is. He?"

"They took him to the lab, that's all I know," he says.

By the time I look up, the other soldiers are on the ground in various states of dead or on their way there.

"Where's the control center?" Thacher growls, pressing his massive foot down on the soldier's stomach.

He cries out again. "Down there. Take a right then left. Can't miss—"

Thacher brings the heel of his foot down on the soldier's face. I stand up, my legs a little wobbly.

"You all right?" Marius asks me, sliding a hand over my waist.

I nod, unable to take my eyes off Thacher. Something wild is still inside of him. I'm relieved he's on our side.

"Let's go," Thacher growls.

Pearl skitters over to us, avoiding the soldiers on the floor.

We're safe for one hallway, but down the next, a flood of soldiers fill the space.

Marius tugs Pearl and me into a room.

Thacher ducks in just as shots fire in the corridor.

I peek from the room, and there are more than a dozen heading our way. We can't go back. If the other soldier told us the truth, we're almost to the control center. To Jack. At least I hope.

"You might want to have that gun ready," I say to Marius.

"What can I do?" Pearl asks.

"Stay here," I say, hoping that we make it through to get her back. If Nerissa finds her, and Jack is still alive and well, then she will use Pearl against him again.

I take a shaky breath as we enter the hallway again. Thacher is in the middle of several soldiers who are trying to take him down.

Marius motions in front of him. He unholsters his gun and leaps onto the soldier closest to him. The others turn and see me.

One soldier tries to hit me, but I duck, shoving my elbow into his side. He reaches for my neck and I twist, wriggling from his grasp. I jab at his face and take him down quickly.

Marius only fires two shots. His aim is true, and two soldiers fall at Thacher's feet, evening the score.

The rest go down quickly.

I call out to Pearl. She sneaks from the room and glues herself to my side.

"Over here," Thacher says, pointing at another map. This one is much clearer.

The soldier had told us the truth, and we head off together, ready for another fight.

Water sloshes under our feet. We're getting closer to the nose of the vessel. My stomach clenches. Jack doesn't have a lot of time.

"In here!" Marius calls.

"Watch out!" Thacher grabs Marius as a jagged piece of metal falls from the ceiling, nearly decapitating him.

I slowly exhale while resting a hand on Marius's shoulder. He looks back and winks.

.

Marius and I walk inside first. There's more smoke than air. I cover my mouth and shut my gills. Though I'm breathing slowly, my heartbeat rushes through my ears.

Thacher moves aside large pieces of metal. "If this is Jack's doing, he made a mess."

I can't help but smile. Until I see a familiar boot, sticking out from one of the metal casings.

"Jack!" I cry and kneel beside the metal. "Marius, help me."

I grip the cylindrical piece and heat scorches my hand. I don't care. I need to help him.

Marius and I lift the debris and place it next to Jack. I fall to his side. He's not moving. Ash covers his face. I touch his cheek. It's not ash. His scorched skin resembles ash. My stomach flips. His eyes are closed, and he's barely breathing.

"We need to get him out of here," I say, choking on my words.

"Jack," Pearl says in the softest voice, falling beside him.

Even though the fire in the room licks at my skin, the burning in my heart gives me the strength to stand up. "She's not getting away with this."

"We can't stay for vengeance," Pearl says. "Jack needs help."

Marius lifts Jack from the floor, gently cradling him in his arms.

I lock eyes with Marius, my heart swelling. "I know. You need to go."

"No," Marius says. "You're coming with us. We have Jack. We can get her some other time. If she's even alive"

"What other time?" I ask. "Look at Jack. She did this to him. I can't let her go. I have to finish this."

"I can't let you go," Marius says, struggling to hold up Jack. I know he wants to drag me out of here, but I won't let him. This is what I've been waiting for. Once Nerissa is gone, this ends for good.

"I won't get another chance."

"She won't be alone," Thacher says.

Marius's face falls. "What are you talking about?"

Thacher takes a deep breath. It rumbles in his throat. "I'm going with her. I'll be able to protect her, son."

Marius props Jack up, and Pearl holds on tight. "Are you sure about this, Sela?"

No, a thousand times no. I never expected to have to take down Nerissa on a sinking vessel. But she's avoided me so far. This might be the last chance I get. She's weak now. It's the perfect time to strike.

"Yes," I say, touching Marius's cheek. He leans into my hand. There isn't time for a sappy goodbye. So, I kiss him on the cheek.

His eyes bore into mine for a moment, as if he's trying to tell me something important. I turn away from him, and Thacher is by my side. We trudge farther into the vessel.

"If she is still on the ship, she's going to be in her lab," Thacher growls.

I nod. Even though his intentions to protect me are sincere, the untamed look in his eyes lets me know he's on a mission to see Nerissa again. The last time he saw her, he was under her control. I'm guessing he has a few *words* for her.

Me too.

We don't come up against any Syndicate soldiers. Most of them are either dead or jumped ship when it went down. We stop at each map, finding our way to her lab quickly. The water is up to my shins—coolness seeping through my suit. There's no reason for us to fear drowning since we can breathe underwater, but that doesn't stop me from worrying that we're too late.

Thacher shoves me down to the floor, and then I hear a *zipping* sound close to my face. Several more follow.

Up ahead, three soldiers walk in formation toward us, their guns aimed and ready. "Stop, there!"

Thacher stands up and charges toward them. Shots pepper his shoulders and legs, but he keeps going. Using his body as a shield, I wait for the opportunity to strike. Thacher grabs one of the soldiers by the throat, and I jump out from behind Thacher's body, punching the first soldier I see. He knocks into the third and they both fall to the ground.

Thacher snaps the other soldier's neck as we approach the other two. One of the men scuffles back into the flooded corridor, trying to fire his weapon again, but he's out of bullets.

"Thacher?" the one closest to me cries out. "How—?"

Thacher quickly silences him.

Kicking my foot out, I knock the last one unconscious. He floats face-up in the water. Maybe he'll wake before the ship goes under. Probably not.

"Come on," Thacher says, stepping over the bodies as if they're furniture.

Then we see her.

Nerissa moves back and forth in front of a desk. Her back is to us. She's shoving equipment into a plastic bin and then whirls around. "I told you, I need a minute—"

Her eyes widen at the sight of us.

My teeth flash. She's so close. I've dreamed of this moment. My hands curl into fists, and I step forward.

Her eyes go wide and her normal put-together appearance is long gone. Her now wild hair sticks out from all angles. "Thacher. Thank goodness you made it."

I stop mid-step. Nerissa hasn't looked at me once. She drops her head into her hands and sobs his name. When she looks up, her makeup has run down her face. She looks frazzled, crazy even. "You've come to help me. Thacher, I knew you would."

CHAPTER 20

Sela

THACHER AND I stand rigid in place for a moment. *Help her?* She turned him into a monster, how could she think he would ever help her again?

I glance at him, making sure we're still on the same page. The last thing I need is for him to fall for her sob story and then turn against me.

"Aren't you going to come over here? I've been so worried," Nerissa says, arms extended. Her tone flips from upset to flirtatious within seconds. She's throwing it all out there to get him back to her side.

Thacher turns to me and shakes his head in disgust.

"After saving you, this is the thanks I get?" Nerissa stands straighter, but her eyes slip to the ground. With all the debris, I can't tell what she's searching for. But I know she's up to something. She hasn't looked at me once, and the slight makes my blood boil. How dare she treat me like nothing after she ruined my life repeatedly?

Her hand flicks to the side, and I'm on top of her before she can grab whatever she's aiming for.

As I wrap my fingers around her neck, I squeeze. Nerissa chokes and sputters. Her arms reach up to hit me, but I block every movement. If I tighten a little more, there will be no more Nerissa. She deserves to suffer, just like every one of her experiments.

Nerissa's eyes flick to Thacher, and her mouth opens, but no words escape. I flash my teeth at her. The need to take her down fills my soul.

As her eyes roll back in her head, a hand grips my shoulder and pulls me away. I try and hold onto her, but Thacher is too strong.

He stands between us. I rub my stinging arm where he grabbed me.

"What are you doing?" My chest constricts. Is he on her side still?

"She needs to know what she's done," he growls and whips around to face her. "I want you to see the monster you created. A shadow of someone you claimed to love all these years. I trusted you, Nerissa. I put you near my son, and all you've brought to the both of us is pain and heartache. You pitted me against Marius, practically ripping my heart from my chest. He's my son, how could you use him to manipulate me like that? What sort of evil lives within you?"

Nerissa's eyes widen as she draws in gulps of air. She glares at me before looking up at Thacher. Her arms lift in surrender. "Everything I've done was for the love I feel for you."

I snort, unable to help it.

Nerissa shoots daggers at me with her eyes. "Jack and Marius are responsible for what you are."

Thacher stiffens, appearing taller than he already is. "What are you talking about?"

Licking her lips, she continues. "Jack shot you. Remember? He wanted you dead—"

"That's not true!" I spat.

Thacher throws his hand out for me to stop talking. He stands between Nerissa and me, so I obey. For now.

"If I didn't intervene, you would have died," Nerissa says. "Marius wanted revenge so badly that he didn't care enough to end his rivalry with Jack to help you. He doesn't love you the way I do. No one does."

Thacher shakes his head so violently that I think his neck is going to snap right off his shoulders. "No!" he bellows.

"I would never pit you against Marius. He's the one who fought you. But I'll never leave you. I love you so much, my dear. I've done this all for us so that we could survive. Together. All we need is the two of us, and we can conquer the world."

Thacher's shoulders rise and fall. His breathing comes out raspy.

"Thacher, don't believe anything she says," I say, trying to calm him down. "She's a liar."

He reaches up and smashes his hands into the closest table, cracking it in half. The computer crashes to the floor. He charges over to the wall, and Nerissa jumps out of his way. He screams and growls and punches his fists against anything he can get his hands on.

We don't have time for this.

I turn to Nerissa, but she's halfway across the room. I don't see the flash of silver until it's too late.

"No!" I scream as she presses the stun gun against his neck.

His back straightens, and then he crumbles to the floor, writhing in pain. She holds the stun device to his neck, giving him dose after dose of electricity. He's enhanced now, but I'm sure her weapon is as well.

I push through the fear of her hitting me with that thing and pounce. Then I smack down on her arm as hard as I can.

Nerissa cries out, and the device clatters to the floor.

Thacher is still, but he's breathing.

More than I can say will be true for her when I'm finished.

Without him to stop me, I grab her by the neck again and shove her against the wall. Her legs kick out from under her, and I add weight to her neck, lifting her off the ground. Her nails scratch against the wall as she tries to take hold of something.

Heat burns through me. This is what I've been waiting for.

"Sela, no," Nerissa says through sputtering breaths. "I did this for everyone."

"You're not feeding me that same line. I'm not Thacher."

She swallows, her throat constricts under my hand. No way I'm budging this time.

"I want to save humanity. The only way we can do that is to advance ourselves. Or else we're going to go extinct. The progress I've made is revolutionary. You're alive because of my experiments. You would have never been able to do the things you do without your abilities."

"Humanity was doing just fine before your experiments," I say through my teeth. I think of all the children who died under her hand. I allow the anger and hatred to fill me. It's the only way I'm going to be able to kill her for good.

"This isn't you, Sela," Nerissa says in a choked whisper. "You don't kill people."

"You don't know anything about me," I say, tightening my grip. It's not enough, though. She's still alive, and I can't bring myself to snap her neck or even choke her to death.

In frustration, my grip falters. What am I doing? *Finish her*, the voice inside of me demands.

I close my eyes, drawing in a fortifying breath.

A rumbling in Nerissa's throat forces my eyes to snap open. A wicked grin crosses her lips.

She's mocking me.

I hold her smug expression in my head, feeding the flames of anger within me. As I clamp down on her throat, a deafening boom fills the room.

I block my face with my arm and, in that split second, Nerissa falls from my grip. Glancing over my shoulder, I expect the worst from the explosion rattling the vessel. Flickering shadows fill the wall outside of the room.

I turn to Nerissa, needing to end this now, but she's gone.

No, not gone. She's on the ground a few feet away.

Before I lunge at her, she whips around, holding the device in her hands. The one that took down Thacher. I have no chance if that thing touches me.

Nerissa shoves her messy hair from her face. The outline of my hand blooms red on her neck. "You stupid girl. I should have taken you out when I had the chance. I won't make that mistake again." Her voice is hoarse.

Letting out a raspy battle cry, she charges me, and I dig my heels in. Her face fills my vision right before I crouch and grab her by the waist. I grip her arm, holding it high enough to keep the device as far away from me as possible.

Nerissa cries out again, her frustrated screams overpowering the moaning of the ship as it struggles to stay afloat.

With everything in me, I shove her against the wall. There's a sickening crunch. I freeze.

A slow breath releases from Nerissa's mouth as the device falls to the floor. Her eyes are wide and her jaw slackens.

Something sharp grazes my arm, and for a second, it looks like she has another weapon. I jump away from her, but she doesn't move away from the wall.

A piece of jagged metal juts out from her stomach.

I clamp a hand over my mouth and turn away as the room tilts at an unnatural angle. The water on the ground darkens with her blood.

With my head spinning and stomach trying to vomit, I grab on to one of the tables and try to hold myself up. Tears blur my vision as the life slips from Nerissa's body. She slumps against the wall. Her chin bows to her chest. Those eyes, which used to hold cockiness and hatred, are now lifeless and glossy.

I inhale several shaky breaths before my shoulders relax. A sound between a sob and a laugh bubbles out of me. She's gone. Our tormentor is dead. Even though I hadn't intended for the scenario to go that way, she's finally gone.

The events of her death play over and over in my head. It was an accident, but the damage from her own vessel killed her. But I helped.

Thacher scrapes his hand against the floor, and I jump up from the table. Glancing at Nerissa, I lick my lips, wondering if there is any way I can ease him into seeing her like that. A thousand excuses flood my mind, but she's still dead, and I'm the one to blame.

"Sela?" he says.

"Over here."

He slowly stands and rubs the part of his neck where Nerissa had hit him with her device. He takes in the room and then sees her. His eyes turn to saucers, and he rushes over to her.

I back away from him as his hands hover over her body.

"She's—she's—" he stammers.

He whirls around to face me, and I grimace, pressing my back against the edge of the table.

"It was an accident. She was going to hit me with that stun gun."

The beast lumbers toward me. Is he about to tear me limb from limb, like he had the rest of the room?

I wince, trying to make myself appear smaller.

I back away, but his arms wrap around my body and pull me closer. I shut my eyes as uncertainty pours over me. Even though Thacher's grip is strong, he doesn't squeeze me to death.

His massive hand pats my back and then moves in smooths slow circles.

It takes me longer than I care to admit to realize that he's hugging me. I sink against his chest as a few tears slip from my eyes.

"It's over," he says, his voice rumbling in his chest.

I nod my head, unable to speak.

The vessel dips to the side, and I lose my footing. Thacher holds me tight until we're able to stand up again.

"We need to leave," he says.

Two more explosions rock the ship. Sickness pools inside of me. I'm not going down with Nerissa. Our mission is complete. Now it's time to save ourselves.

Thacher crosses the room and peers into the hallway. He grips the door frame as one more explosion shoots debris against the walls outside.

"Come on, Sela," he says and charges from the room.

I take one more look at Nerissa and her lifeless body that's attached to the wall. Good riddance. The world is a better place without someone like her.

I walk toward the doorway when something catches my eye. In the box that Nerissa frantically packed, a small black device peeks out from the top. I pick up the device; the edges are smooth, and a tugging from deep within me knows this piece of equipment is important. I hold it against my chest as I sprint from the room.

Thacher calls out for me, and I follow his voice. There aren't any more lights illuminating our way. Water rushes over the floors and, by the time I reach him, my legs ache with the movement.

"It's completely flooded down there," Thacher says.

I tuck the small black box into my suit, securing it in place. "I suppose it's a good thing we're both good swimmers."

He doesn't smile. "We need to get away from the vessel entirely. There's too much debris for us to be safe. Stick by my side, OK?"

I swallow against the lump in my throat. "OK."

The ship pitches to the side, and Thacher and I crash against the wall again. We're no longer able to walk as the water is too high. Instead, I go underwater and start to swim. The water dulls the sounds around me, and I'm able to concentrate on the task at hand. Thacher wasn't kidding about the debris. With the vessel fully submerged, it's like an obstacle course of floating equipment, broken shards of metal, and other dangerous objects not meant for the ocean. I let out a few sonar clicks to avoid getting pummeled.

We stop at a map, which miraculously is still attached to a wall. I grab onto Thacher's arm as he presses his finger against the directions, showing our new path.

I shove away from the wall and head toward the next hallway. If we have the directions correct, we should come to an escape hatch at the end of this corridor.

The *should* turns to *can't* as debris blocks our way. Thacher and I pull at the large piece of metal, but it's jammed against both sides of the hallway. There isn't enough space for either of us to pass through.

Thacher and I face each other. The corners of his mouth tug downward. I shake my head and signal for him to follow me back down the hallway.

I curse at myself for staying with Nerissa for as long as we did. If I took her down sooner, we would have been out of this ship by now.

Each corridor ends abruptly as the debris piles up.

Thacher waves his hand at me, and I lock eyes with him. He points downward. I struggle to understand what he means. He swirls his finger and points down again.

"New plan," he mouths.

I nod. Forcing ourselves against the water current to reach the surface isn't working anymore. The debris is floating upward, blocking our exits. If we push to the bottom of the vessel, there's a chance we'll be able to escape.

We swim together, and the corridors closer to the bottom of the ocean don't present as many obstacles. We peer into each room, looking for portals big enough to get Thacher through.

It doesn't take us long and we discover a massive room where the windows are bigger than Nerissa's lab. Thacher grabs two pieces of metal, and hands one to me. We go to the edge of the window, and he shoves the edge of his piece into the corner. He presses down on the other end to shimmy the hatch free.

I shove my metal piece into the space that Thacher created and push against it. Between our enhanced strength and the pressure of the water, the glass cracks and snaps free from the frame.

Thacher motions for me to go first, and I do.

Streams of light guide us. We push hard and reach the surface. When I break through, the sun scorches my eyes. I blink away the black dots in my vision. And then I see the back of the flying vessel now completely submerged under the water.

Something jerks me under the water. Something so strong that I'm unable to swim forward. Then I realize what's happening. The suction of the ship is pulling me down in its quick descent to the ocean floor. I kick as hard as I can and reach for the surface. The force pulling at me is strong, but I'm stronger.

A form floats nearby. Thacher. He's pushing through the suction too. I pump my arms, bringing me closer to him.

He grabs my hand and tugs me upward. His strength overpowers the sinking ship and, once again, I reach the surface.

He comes up seconds later. But we're not out of danger yet. We quickly swim away from the ship and into calmer waters.

The *Echelon* is farther in the distance. The ocean must have pulled Nerissa's vessel farther away during its descent into the watery depths.

A motor starts and the skiff buzzes in our direction. I wave my hands in the air so that they can see us. Marius stands at the controls, but I don't see Jack anywhere. Pearl's head bobs up and my pulse spikes. She would never leave Jack.

Thacher and I swim over, and I climb inside of the boat. Jack lays unconscious on one side. Red, blotchy skin covers his body, but he's healing.

I finally take an easy breath.

Red veins fill what should be the white parts of Pearl's eyes. She's inhaling shuddering breaths, trying to regulate her self-control. Her emotions mirror the storm inside of me. But there's no time to freak out. I must remain strong.

"It's over," Thacher says.

Marius kneels beside me and takes my hand. I raise my eyes to him, but I can't utter the words. I killed her. Sure, she was the evilest human on the planet, but I'm still unsure of how to deal with my actions.

Marius glances at Thacher and nods. He doesn't need me to say the words aloud, and I silently thank him for that. He squeezes my shoulder to reassure me.

Thacher climbs aboard, and Marius and I hold Jack in place. His head lolls to the side, and Pearl cups his cheeks to keep him steady.

"Let's get him back to the *Echelon*," I say.

Pearl scoots over, giving Thacher more room, and I join Marius at the controls.

The boat takes a sharp turn to the right, and Marius glances my way and asks, "You alright?"

"No," I say. "But eventually I will be."

I know he wants to ask more, but I'm thankful he doesn't.

Once we reach the *Echelon*, several of the crew take Jack and Pearl to the med bay.

Papa's warship remains in the distance. The entire time, it just sat there, watching Jack's capture and my rescue. So much for Papa caring about my friends or me.

As I cross the deck, a loud horn rips through the air. I whip around toward the source, for a split-second thinking that Papa wants to relay a message to me. But I'm wrong. The warship descends into the water, hiding as he had this entire time. Papa leaves without another word. As hurt as I am, I'm not sure what I would say to him if he tried, anyway.

My insides twist at the thought of him sacrificing so many innocent children for his gain. I wonder if he will ever learn.

I shove thoughts of him aside and jog downstairs toward the med bay.

Pearl sits next to Jack's bed. He's still out, and a line in his arm is currently feeding him fluids. From the steady rise and fall of his chest, I know he'll be OK soon.

Pearl glances over my shoulder toward the door. "Is Marius coming down?"

I shake my head. "He's the captain now. We're on a course back to Avalon." I smile to myself at the thought. I'm still reeling from Nerissa's death. But there's no reason to fight anymore, but the hard work isn't over. We have a lot of pieces to clean up.

"I wanted to thank you, for everything," Pearl says, wringing her hands together.

"Don't worry about it," I say.

She steps forward and takes my hands in hers. "You didn't just save Jack's life. You saved mine. I'm so sorry that you lost Una. I'm grateful, but I feel awful that you might have lost her because you saved me first." Tears spill out of her eyes and roll down her cheeks.

"Hey," I say and then fold her into an embrace. I didn't realize how much I needed a hug. Grief over Una's death stirs in my chest, and it's so nice to feel comforted by another.

Things are going to be OK now.

Pearl backs away and smiles at me as she wipes the tears from her face. "I can't stop crying."

"Today was a rough one," I say with a smile.

She laughs. "No kidding."

We walk over to Jack and sit together, hand-in-hand. I want to see him when he wakes up and be the first to tell him our fight with Nerissa is finally over.

As we get closer to Avalon, I join Marius on the bridge. I long to see Marin and Talise, even though I must inform them that we lost another Sister. The radar shows we're near the settlement. I look forward to sharing with everyone that Nerissa is dead and the threat to our survival is finally over.

"What is *that*?" one of the crew members asks.

I look up from the screens and gasp. Several vessels rocket toward us as the radio crackles to life.

"Hello?" Marin's voice fills the cabin. "Sela. Marius. Anyone?"

I grab the comm from the operations panel. "Marin? It's Sela. What's going on?"

Something grabs my attention on the horizon. Black smoke fills the sky directly above Avalon.

"Nerissa has a flying vessel," Marin says, her voice thick with emotion. "We didn't stand a chance. The settlement is sinking. Nothing is left other than what we were able to salvage on these boats."

Only four fighting vessels and two repurposed cruise liners approach us.

"There was no way to counter her attack from the sky," Marin continues after radio silence from my end. I don't have any words for what I'm seeing. I wish Jack was well enough to fly over there and save some others. But it's too dangerous for anyone.

I sag against Marius, and he squeezes me against him. He takes the comm from me and tells her what I did. How we took down Nerissa. I barely hear their conversation over the rush of blood in my ears.

It wasn't enough for Nerissa to have Jack. Her final act of evil didn't give anyone the opportunity to defy her.

"Is Jack there?" Marin asks.

"He's injured," Marius says.

"Oh," she says.

I grab the device, knowing something is wrong. "What happened, Marin?" If Jack lost his friends because of Nerissa, I want to know so I can soften the blow.

"His Forgotten Boys are on our ship, but Coral didn't make it."

Our vessels are anchored close to each other as we piece together the devastation. The survivors of Avalon work together to help the injured and gather all the supplies from the settlement's salvaged inventory. We learn thousands of civilians and crew died in the fight, leaving us with little. A deep sadness fills the area.

I barely move from my post on the bridge. The other ships radio in, giving us updates about their injured passengers and the supplies they were able to save from Avalon. I want to know everything and help in any way I can. My remaining Sisters are now safe and staying with Marius gives me purpose.

"Sela!" Ethan calls from behind.

With the strength I have left, I turn to him. "What?"

Elijah bursts through the door next to Ethan and nearly topples over. He grabs onto a chair, panting.

I raise an eyebrow.

"You need to get out of your workstation more often," Ethan says, clapping a hand on Elijah's back.

Elijah's eyes brighten as he pushes his glasses farther up the bridge of his nose and looks at me. "The device you gave me. I've cracked the encryption."

I walk over to them and cross my arms. "What was on it?"

Elijah and Ethan share a look. I'm about to put my foot down when Elijah speaks.

"When Pearl's parents were on their scouting mission all those years back, they discovered a potential land location."

"Are you serious?" I ask.

"It looks like Nerissa was the one to capture their vessel and stole the data, killing her parents in the process."

"Does Pearl know?" Marius asks, coming to my side.

"You're the first person we've told about this," Ethan says. "Pearl is a little preoccupied."

"And very emotional," Elijah adds.

"If Nerissa knew about this," I say, "then she probably wanted to exploit the land to expand her control of the world."

"Now that she's dead, and we have this information, we could take it," Marius says. "With Avalon gone, we don't have many options."

Without Nerissa in the way, we could start anew on real land. If her data is real, that is. Who knows what this new location has in store for us.

Everyone thought the oceans had consumed all the land, but this information could change everything.

The thought of soft, sand-filled beaches that my toes dig into floods my mind. Somewhere to call home. I've lived on drifting vessels for far too long and, before that, I was deep under the ocean, far from the warmth of the sun.

"What does it say about the landmass location?" Marius asks, stepping next to me.

I snap from my fantasies and refocus.

Elijah taps away at the display, eagerly scanning the data. "Most of the files are corrupt and a lot of the docs are redacted, but I am sure I can piece this together if given enough time."

A smile pulls on my lips. Water is all I've known. Land isn't what I'm designed for, but there's still a yearning inside of me, a longing to find something more— something better. It could all be a dream—a myth—but what do we have to lose? We can float aimlessly on the sea, eventually running out of supplies. Or we can take a chance.

"I think we should find it," I say. "We've lost so much. Time for us to live—not just survive."

EPILOGUE

Sela

I LEAN ONTO the railing of the *Echelon* and peer out over the silvery horizon. Wind plays with my hair, and I watch as wispy, red strands float free about my face. The air in my chest grows tight with every breath. I thought I would feel free with our search for land, now that Nerissa is dead. But I don't. Even after three months, I still sometimes wake up with nightmares of how I failed Una and Derya—failed to save them. I miss my Sisters every day and would give anything to hear Una's voice—even if she were just bossing me around.

I need to find peace.

The Terran Sea laps up onto the hull, catching my attention. Inviting as ever, the ocean slaps the vessel's surface as the blue water rises and falls. The familiar sound settles over me, calling my mood as I draw in a long breath of the briny air. The rest of the ships salvaged from Avalon, including the *Sarus,* trail behind ours, carrying those who wanted to see if the legend of land was true. But the people who were held captive by Nerissa decided to remain behind in a place once familiar—Atlantis. Dad welcomed them back for as long as they please, including Talise, who needed a break from adventuring. At least Marin came through and is now in charge of the *Sarus.* As for me, I am taking a break from playing captain for a while.

Marius steps in close from behind, slipping his warm hand around my waist. The other hand—the one Jack chopped off—wouldn't be nearly as warm. But the replacement is a perfect match to the original. Well, except for the body heat. Elijah made the prosthetic, of course. He really is a genius. And the one who also decrypted most of Nerissa's data on finding a potential land mass, including the general coordinates. But the ocean is a big place. Land probably doesn't exist anyway.

I snuggle into the safety of Marius's muscular body, and he pulls me in tight.

"Thinking again?" he asks.

"Oh, you know me. Always trying to run through the plans in my head." I look up to his smiling face and brilliant blue eyes. I've loved Marius for as long as I can remember, and I never want my love for him to end.

He presses his lips to the side of my head, and a shiver shimmies down my spine with his kiss. "That's one reason

I love you," he whispers. "You're always ready for the next adventure."

I smile. "What's the other reason?"

"Your fiery temperament," he says without missing a beat.

I chuckle, spin in his arms, and then stand on my toes for another kiss—a real one this time.

"Hope I'm not interrupting anything?" Jack's now very annoying voice sounds from nearby.

I whip my neck toward him and shoot a vicious glare in his direction. But the warning does little to warn him off. Jack struts toward us wearing a stupid grin. Marius separates from me slightly, leveling a look of his own at Jack.

"Flynn, I'm sure you have more important tasks than to be bothering us," Marius drones.

Jack sidles up on my other side and then pats me on the head. "I just missed Sela . . . and I'm a little bored with forever sailing." He lets out a long, fake sigh.

I whack his hand away with a scowl. But my unfortunate best friend holds my stare and continues, his goofy smile still in place. His hair sticks up in random places, styled as if by rolling out of bed. After a few seconds, I break into a laugh and sock Jack in the arm. "I can't stay mad at you. You're too dumb."

Jack rubs at the spot I hit for a little longer than he should.

I reach out to tame his hair, but it really needs a proper combing, and there's no use. "You're letting yourself go. What will Pearl think?"

But before Jack answers, a screech comes from the way of the ocean. My heart jumps at the unknown sound. Nearly in unison, the three of us whip toward the noise.

In the distance, a white object hovers in the air above the water. The creature looks to be a couple of feet wide when flapping its wings to stay afloat. Hope bubbles inside of me.

"Is that bird what I think it is?" I ask, my voice breathy with excitement. "Because that could mean . . ."

"Pretty sure it's a gull, all right," Jack cuts me off. "I would fly out there to check, but I don't want to scare the thing."

I punch Jack in the arm again. "You really are softening up these days."

Marius lets out a hearty laugh and then pulls a comm from his pocket, clicking the button. "Ethan."

"What's up?"

"Put Tug at the helm and get down to the bow of the ship," Marius says. "There's something you need to see."

Ethan laughs, "He'll like that. I'll be right down."

A few moments later, Ethan and Pearl gaze out over the water and watch as another bird joins the first, both now soaring over our ship.

"Don't get too excited," Ethan says. "I read that these birds were known to sometime fly up to ten thousand miles from land."

"Ten thousand?" Marius asks.

"But they usually stay within one hundred or less," Pearl adds. "Meaning we could be close."

One of the gulls, with white and gray feathers, lands on the rail and squawks.

"Well, that's an unattractive sound," Jack says while furrowing his brows, clearly not enamored with the creature anymore.

Pearl catches his arm. "Oh, it's not so bad. You'll get used to it." She kisses Jack on the cheek. If it were possible, I think he would melt into a puddle.

Ethan's eyes light up, and then he clicks off his comm. "I have to get back up. Tug has something on the radar . . ."

"We're going too." I swing my attention around to the others, my heart racing.

Ethan waves his hand in the air. "Most likely it's just an excuse to switch places with me, so he can come down and feed the bird."

"You just don't want to get your hopes up," I scold Ethan.

He shrugs. "Just stay down here. I'll call you if there's any news.

From my side, Jack eyes the gull as the bird steps along the rail, inching closer to us. He lets out a squawk and flaps his arms, but the beast only does the same and maintains its new territory. Pearl pulls Jack away from the bird and then pilots him to the other side of the ship. Jack will probably get used to all the new sights and sounds that land has to offer sooner than most of us. I'm not sure our new life will be easy, but we'll all transition eventually. Even me.

I huff an irritated sigh.

Ethan's practical mindset is frustrating. He may be right, though. We could be getting our hopes up too soon. I grab Marius's hand and lead him toward the front of the bow. In the meantime, we can keep a lookout and wait for Ethan's comm.

But it's not long before a dot appears on the horizon— one I hadn't seen before. My pulse thrums in my ears at the sight.

"You think that's land?" I ask, my hands shaking.

Marius raises his comm, but I'm unable to control myself. I snatch the device from him.

"Ethan is that land dead ahead?" I demand into the device, and as soon as I get the words out, Jack and Pearl are right behind us.

"Tug really did have something on his radar." Ethan's now high-pitched voice crackles through loud and clear. "That's definitely a large land mass."

Jack lets out a whoop and sweeps Pearl off her feet. Her sweet laugh surrounds us as she hugs him tight while he swings her in flamboyant circles. Apparently disgusted with all the celebratory commotion, the gull flaps its wings and launches into the air.

"Time to destination?" I ask Ethan.

The ship kicks into full speed toward the dot on the horizon.

"Estimates are two hours," Ethan says and clicks off.

"Two hours?" I say to Marius. "I don't know if I can wait that long."

But the four of us do wait—what else can we do? We spend plenty of time bugging Ethan and Tug in the cockpit. But Ethan only shoos us away and tells us to find something else to do.

Eventually, a hazy mountain range comes into view with sprawling, white sand skirting its base. Squinting and leaning forward, I peer into lush, green foliage covering every inch of the mountainside—the kind of vegetation I've only seen in my studies. My heart picks up the pace, and my breath shortens.

"Dry land," Pearl whispers to my side.

I look to her and smile, and she returns the expression.

But in a flash, Jack sweeps Pearl off her feet again and takes to the air. "See you guys there." They zip across the sky while I hear her shouting, "Don't you drop me!"

"You going overboard too?" Marius asks, looking over the side of the ship.

I gaze down at the tempting waves below, and a bit of longing stirs in my stomach. But then I return my attention to Marius and wrap my arms around his neck.

Smiling, I stretch up to his ear and whisper, "Nope. When I take my first steps onto the new world, I want you right there, by my side."

The End

VIP List: Sign up to read exclusive Nerissa, Syndicate log entries and learn more about her ruthless takeover of the Syndicate and how her experimental program began. You will also get updates on the series. In addition, get free content, giveaway opportunities, and other exclusive bonuses by joining our VIP List at tormentpublishing.com.

Thank you for reading Limitless, book one of the Terran Sea Chronicles. If you enjoyed reading this book, please remember to leave a review on Amazon. Positive reviews are the best way to thank an author for writing a book you loved. When a book has a lot of reviews, Amazon will show that book to more potential readers. The review doesn't have to be long—one or two sentences are just fine! We read all our reviews and appreciate each one of them!

www.tormentpublishing.com

Acknowledgements:
Special thanks to Torment Publishing! Without you this book would not have happened. We love you guys. Thanks to all the early readers and the support of our fans.
Thanks to all our family for the support!

Credits:
Chase Night – Editor
Jesikah Sundin - Editor
Jack Llartin – Editor

41399140R00139

Made in the USA
Middletown, DE
06 April 2019